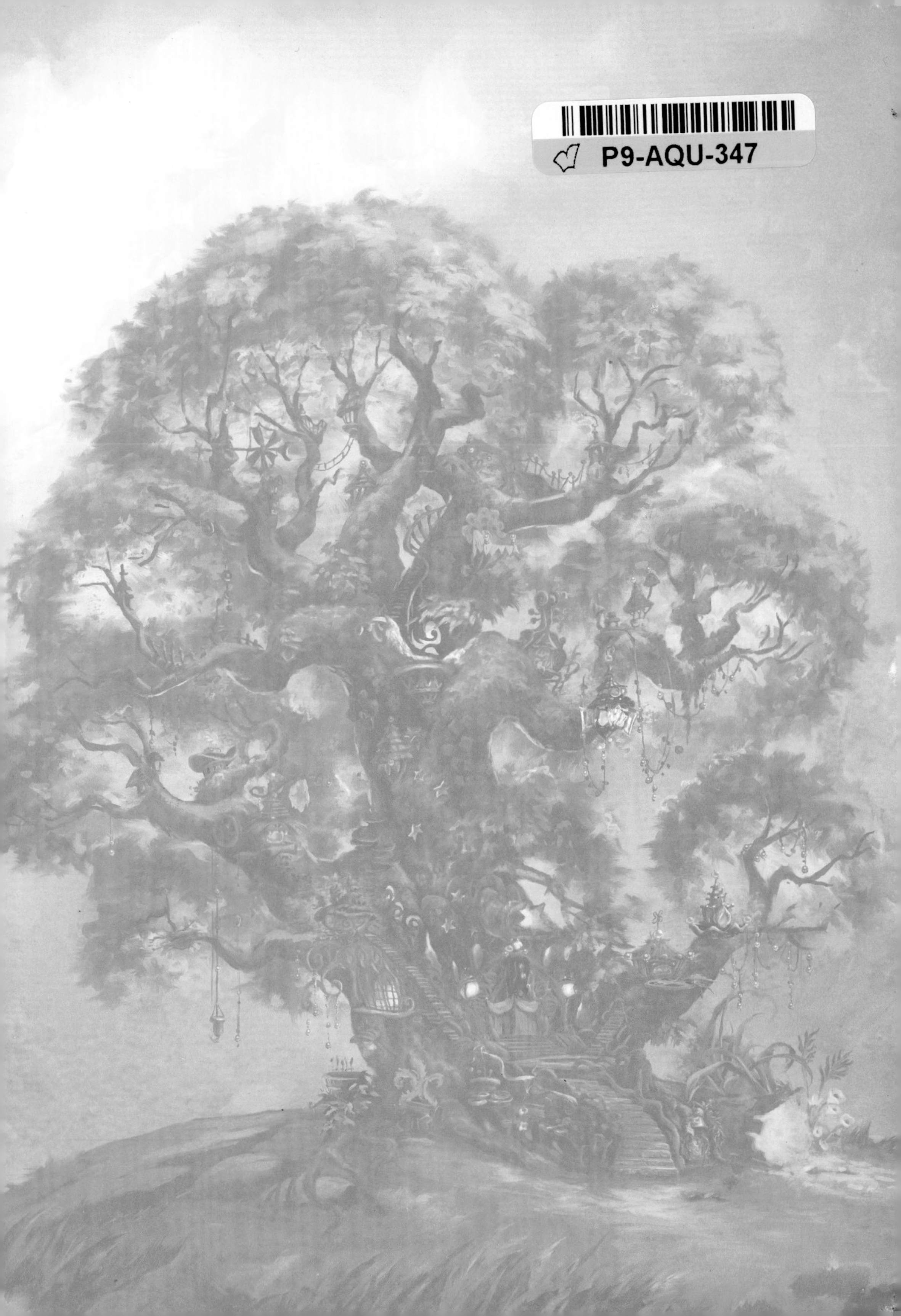

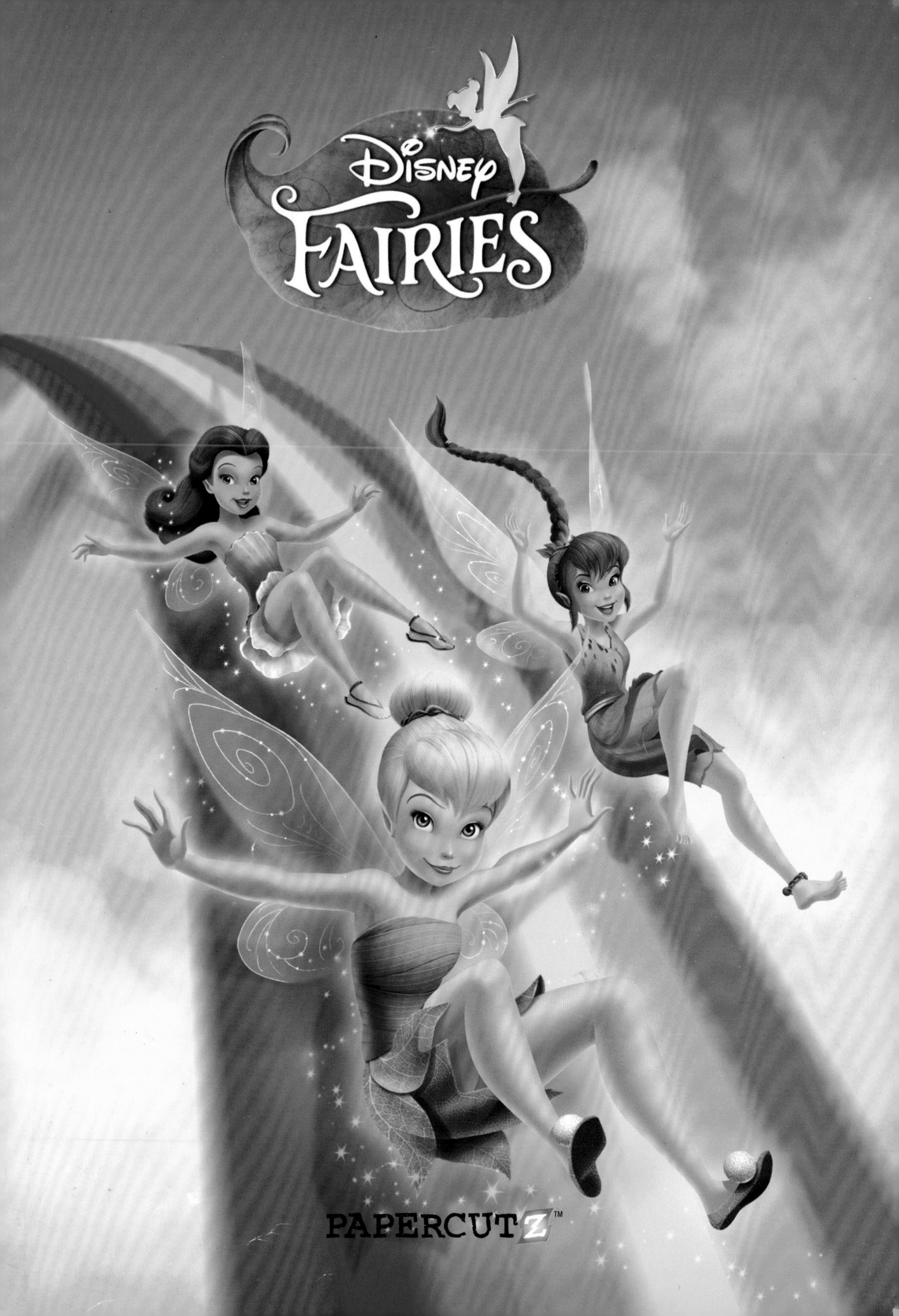
Disney
FAIRIES
PAPERCUTZ™

Disney Fairies

Graphic Novels Available from

PAPERCUTZ

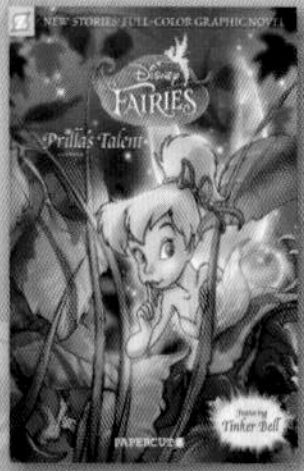

Graphic Novel #1
"Prilla's Talent"

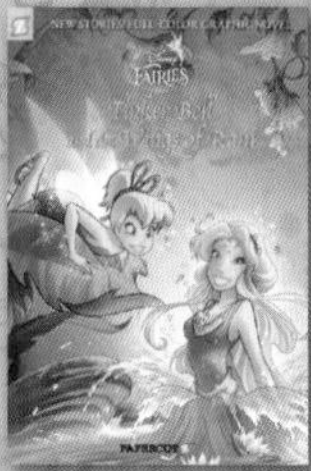

Graphic Novel #2
"Tinker Bell and the Wings of Rani"

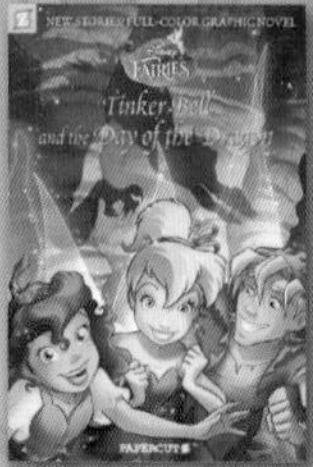

Graphic Novel #3
"Tinker Bell and the Day of the Dragon"

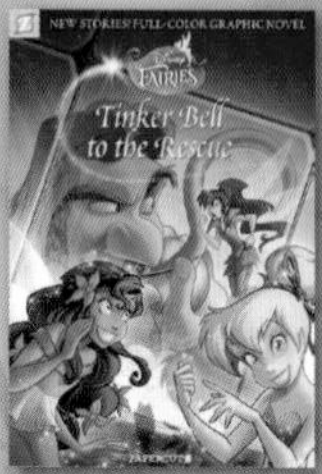

Graphic Novel #4
"Tinker Bell to the Rescue"

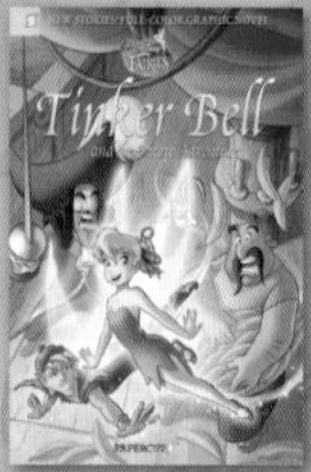

Graphic Novel #5
"Tinker Bell and the Pirate Adventure"

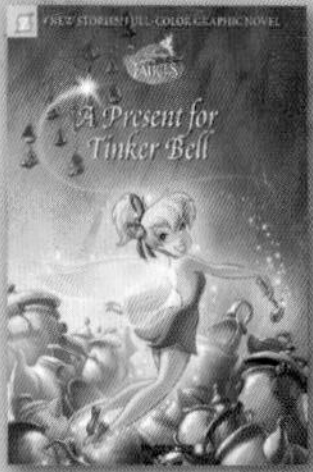

Graphic Novel #6
"A Present for Tinker Bell"

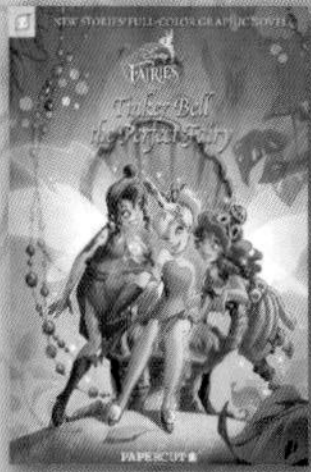

Graphic Novel #7
"Tinker Bell the Perfect Fairy"

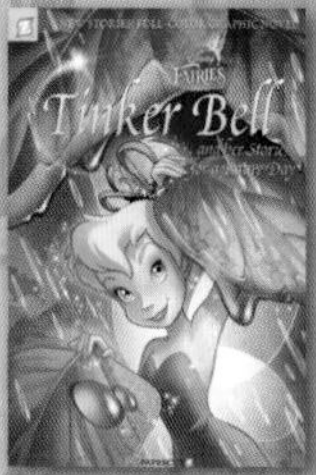

Graphic Novel #8
"Tinker Bell and her Stories for a Rainy Day"

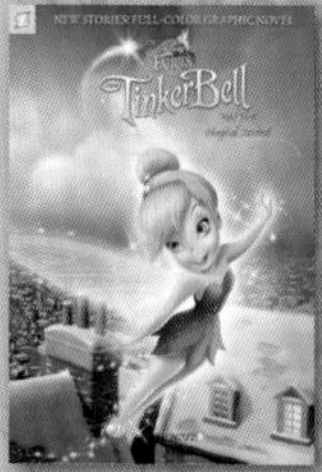

Graphic Novel #9
"Tinker Bell and her Magical Arrival"

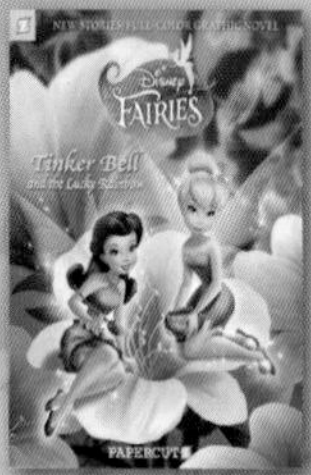

Graphic Novel #10
"Tinker Bell and the Lucky Rainbow"

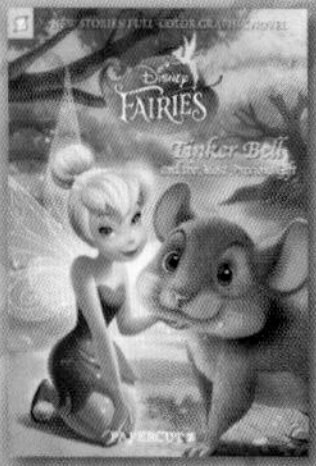

Graphic Novel #11
"Tinker Bell and the Most Precious Gift"

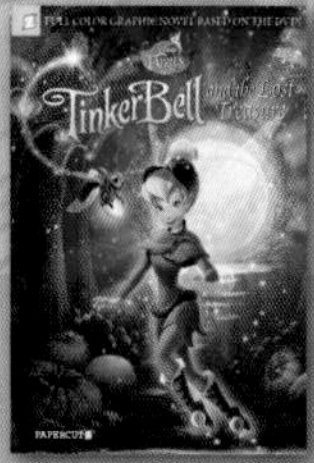

Graphic Novel #12
"Tinker Bell and the Lost Treasure"

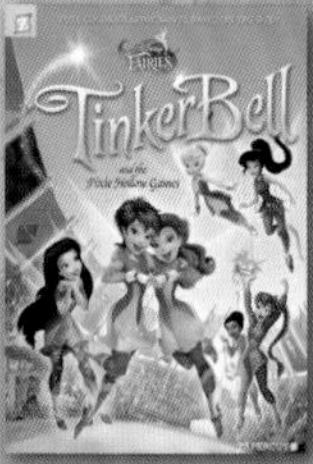

Graphic Novel #13
"Tinker Bell and the Pixie Hollow Games"

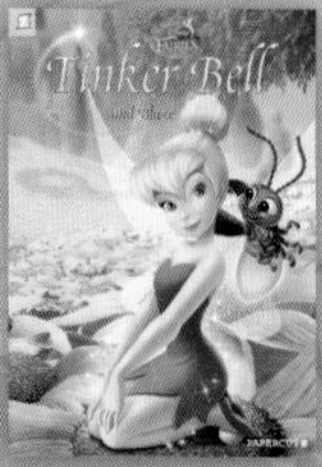

Graphic Novel #14
"Tinker Bell and Blaze"

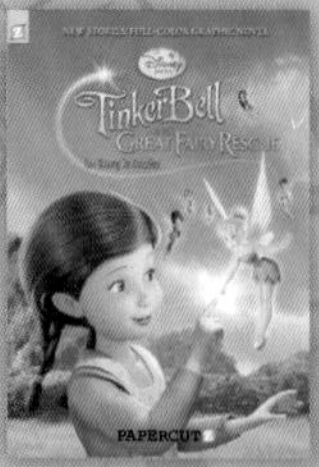

Tinker Bell and the Great Fairy Rescue

COMING SOON

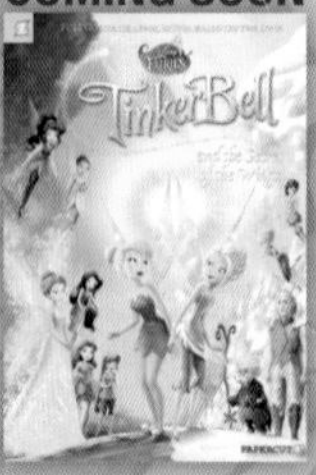

Graphic Novel #15
"Tinker Bell and the Secret of the Wings"

DISNEY FAIRIES graphic novels are available in paperback for $7.99 each; in hardcover for $12.99 each except #5, $6.99PB, $10.99HC. #6-15 are $7.99PB $11.99HC. Tinker Bell and the Great Fairy Rescue is $9.99 in hardcover only.
Available at booksellers everywhere.

See more at papercutz.com

Or you can order from us: Please add $4.00 for postage and handling for first book, and add $1.00 for each additional book. Please make check payable to NBM Publishing. Send to: Papercutz, 160 Broadway, Suite 700, East Wing, New York, NY 10038 or call 800 886 1223 (9-6 EST M-F) MC-Visa-Amex accepted.

#14 "Tinker Bell and Blaze"

Contents

PAPERCUTZ

NEW YORK

"Once Upon a Time"
Script: Emanuela Portipiano
Revised Dialogue: Cortney Faye Powell
Pencils: Manuela Razzi
Inks: Roberta Zanotta
Color: Studio Kawaii
Letters: Janice Chiang
Page 5 Art:
Concept: Tea Orsi
Layout: Monica Catalano
Pencils: Marino Gentile
Color: Andrea Cagol

"Remember Me"
Script: Tea Orsi
Revised Dialogue: Cortney Faye Powell
Pencils: Caterina Giorgilli
Inks: Roberta Zanotta
Color: Studio Kawaii
Letters: Janice Chiang
Page 10 Art:
Concept: Tea Orsi
Pencils and Inks: Sara Storino
Color: Andrea Cagol

"Misunderstood Style"
Script: Tea Orsi
Revised Dialogue: Cortney Faye Powell
Pencils: Manuela Razzi
Inks: Roberta Zanotta
Color: Studio Kawaii
Letters: Janice Chiang

"The Shiny Thing"
Script: Carlo Panaro
Revised Dialogue: Cortney Faye Powell
Pencils: Manuela Razzi
Inks: Roberta Zanotta
Color: Studio Kawaii
Letters: Janice Chiang

"A Fast-flying Fairy Shows her True Colors"
Script: Carlo Panaro
Revised Dialogue: Cortney Faye Powell
Pencils and Inks: Monica Catalano
Color: Studio Kawaii
Letters: Janice Chiang
Page 23 Art:
Layout, Pencils and Inks: Sara Storino
Color: Andrea Cagol

"The Missing Butterfly"
Script: Tea Orsi
Revised Dialogue: Cortney Faye Powell
Pencils and Inks: Monica Catalano
Color: Studio Kawaii
Letters: Janice Chiang

"The Bad Mannered Blossom"
Script: Tea Orsi
Revised Dialogue: Cortney Faye Powell
Pencils: Manuela Razzi
Inks: Marina Baggio
Color: Studio Kawaii
Letters: Janice Chiang
Page 32 Art:
Concept: Caterina Giorgetti
Pencils and Inks: Sara Storino
Color: Andrea Cagol

"False Alarm!"
Script: Emanuela Portipiano
Revised Dialogue: Cortney Faye Powell
Pencils: Sara Storino
Inks: Roberta Zanotta
Color: Studio Kawaii
Letters: Janice Chiang
Page 37 Art:
Pencils & Inks: Marino Gentile &
Sara Storino
Color: Mara Damiani &
Stefano Attardi

"A Strange, Strange Star"
Script: Tea Orsi
Revised Dialogue: Cortney Faye Powell
Pencils: Manuela Razzi
Inks: Roberta Zanotta
Color: Studio Kawaii
Letters: Janice Chiang
Page 42 Art:
Concept: Tea Orsi
Pencils and Inks: Sara Storino
Color: Andrea Cagol

"The Long, Long Night"
Script: Emanuela Portipiano
Revised Dialogue: Cortney Faye Powell
Pencils: Manuela Razzi
Inks: Roberta Zanotta
Color: Studio Kawaii
Letters: Janice Chiang
Page 47 Art:
Concept: Tea Orsi
Pencils and Inks: Sara Storino
Color: Andrea Cagol

"A Starless Night"
Script: Carlo Panaro
Revised Dialogue: Cortney Faye Powell
Pencils: Sara Storino
Inks: Roberta Zanotta
Color: Studio Kawaii
Letters: Janice Chiang
Page 52 Art:
Concept: Tea Orsi
Pencils and Inks: Sara Storino
Color: Andrea Cagol

"An Unexpected Adventure"
Script: Carlo Panaro
Revised Dialogue: Cortney Faye Powell
Pencils: Mario Gentile
Inks: Roberta Zanotta
Color: Studio Kawaii
Letters: Janice Chiang
Page 57 Art:
Concept: Tea Orsi
Pencils and Inks: Sara Storino
Color: Andrea Cagol

Production – Dawn K. Guzzo
Special Thanks – Sara Srisoonthorn
Production Coordinator – Beth Scorzato
Associate Editor – Michael Petranek
Jim Salicrup
Editor-in-Chief

ISBN: 978-1-59707-488-9 paperback edition
ISBN: 978-1-59707-489-6 hardcover edition

Printed in China
April 2014 by Asia One Printing LTD
13/F Asia One Tower
8 Fung Yip St., Chaiwan
Hong Kong

Papercutz books may be purchased for business or promotional use. For information on bulk purchases please contact Macmillan Corporate and Premium Sales Department at (800) 221-7945 x5442.

Distributed by Macmillan
First Papercutz Printing

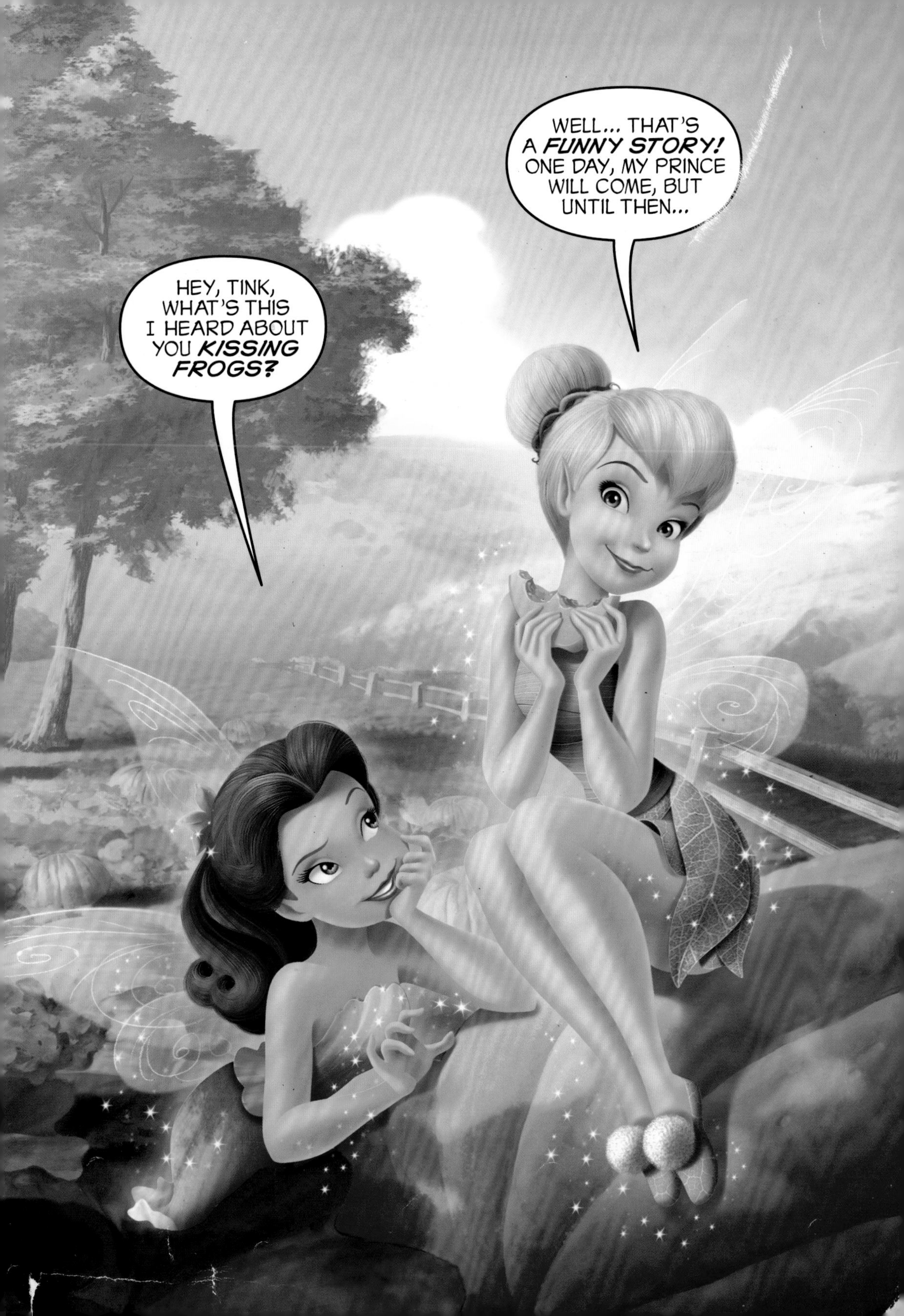
HEY, TINK, WHAT'S THIS I HEARD ABOUT YOU *KISSING FROGS?*
WELL... THAT'S A *FUNNY STORY!* ONE DAY, MY PRINCE WILL COME, BUT UNTIL THEN...

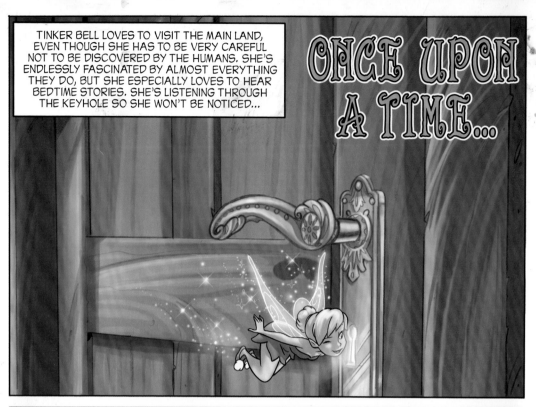

TINKER BELL LOVES TO VISIT THE MAIN LAND, EVEN THOUGH SHE HAS TO BE VERY CAREFUL NOT TO BE DISCOVERED BY THE HUMANS. SHE'S ENDLESSLY FASCINATED BY ALMOST EVERYTHING THEY DO, BUT SHE ESPECIALLY LOVES TO HEAR BEDTIME STORIES. SHE'S LISTENING THROUGH THE KEYHOLE SO SHE WON'T BE NOTICED...

ONCE UPON A TIME...

...AND SO, THE PRINCESS *KISSED* THE FROG, WHO TURNED INTO A HANDSOME *PRINCE!*

WOW!

AND THEY LIVED HAPPILY EVER AFTER!

HOW ROMANTIC!

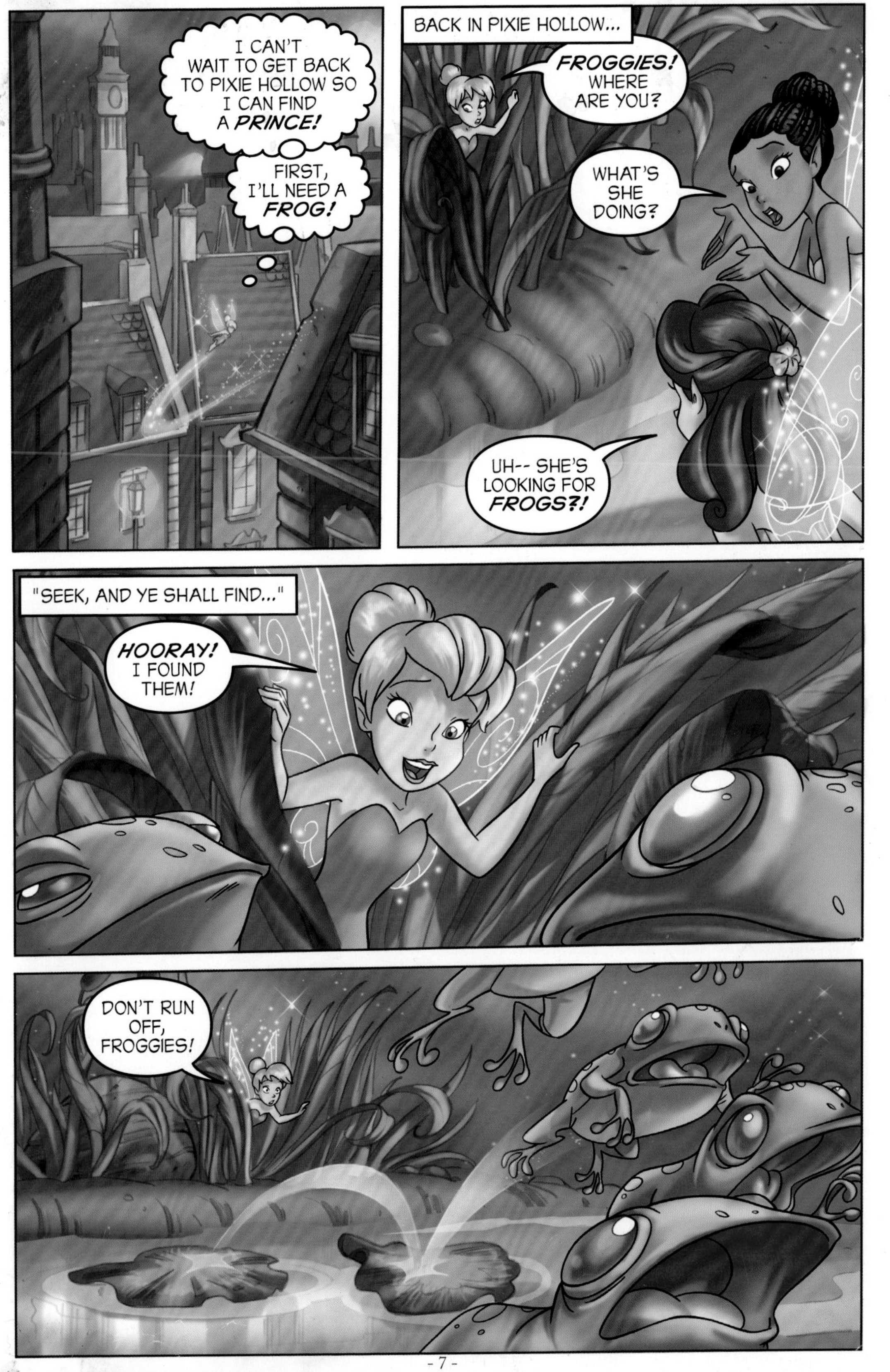
I CAN'T WAIT TO GET BACK TO PIXIE HOLLOW SO I CAN FIND A *PRINCE!*
FIRST, I'LL NEED A *FROG!*
BACK IN PIXIE HOLLOW...
FROGGIES! WHERE ARE YOU?
WHAT'S SHE DOING?
UH-- SHE'S LOOKING FOR *FROGS?!*
"SEEK, AND YE SHALL FIND..."
HOORAY! I FOUND THEM!
DON'T RUN OFF, FROGGIES!

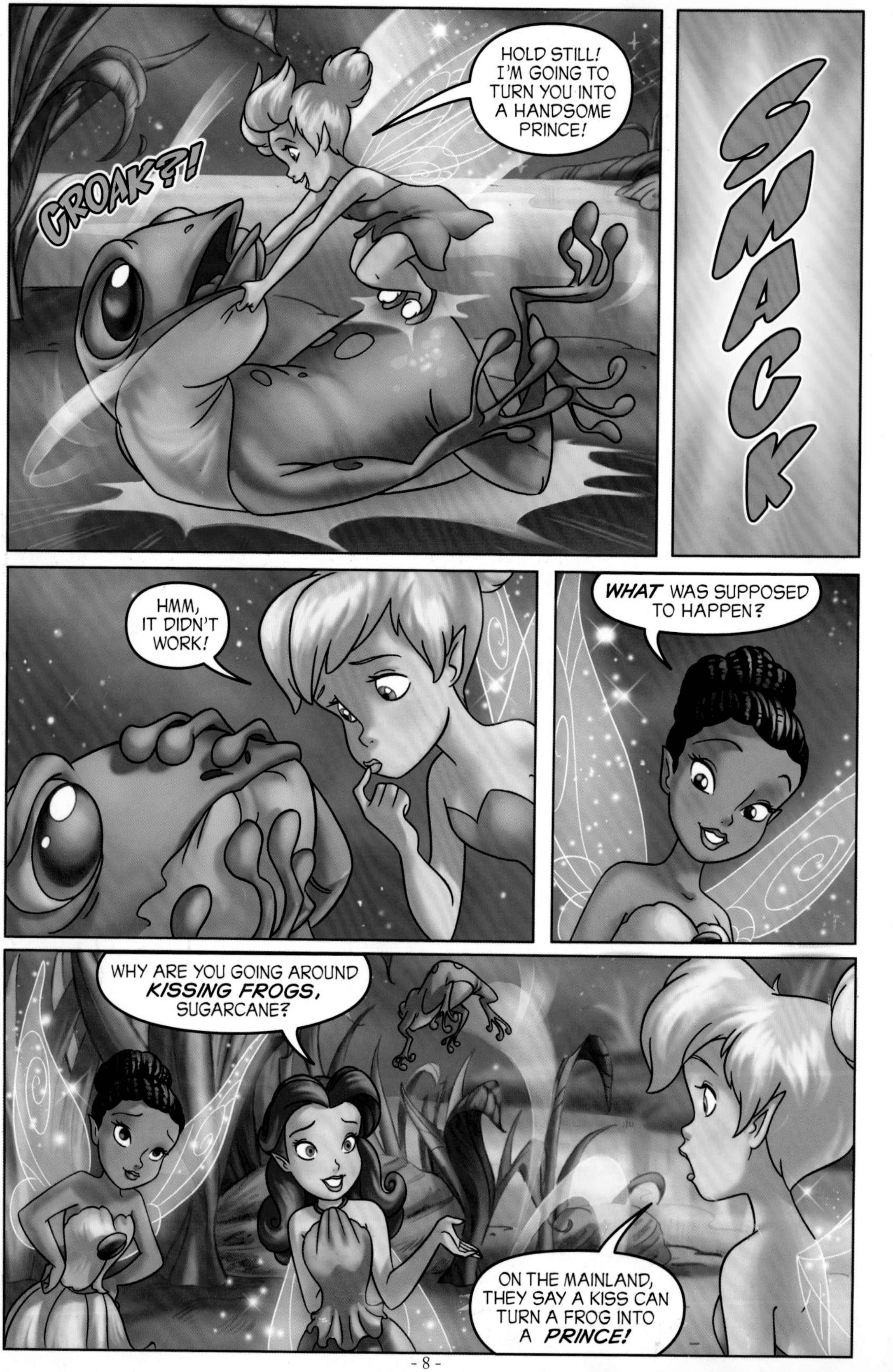
HOLD STILL! I'M GOING TO TURN YOU INTO A HANDSOME PRINCE!
CROAK?!
SMACK
HMM, IT DIDN'T WORK!
WHAT WAS SUPPOSED TO HAPPEN?
WHY ARE YOU GOING AROUND *KISSING FROGS,* SUGARCANE?
ON THE MAINLAND, THEY SAY A KISS CAN TURN A FROG INTO A *PRINCE!*

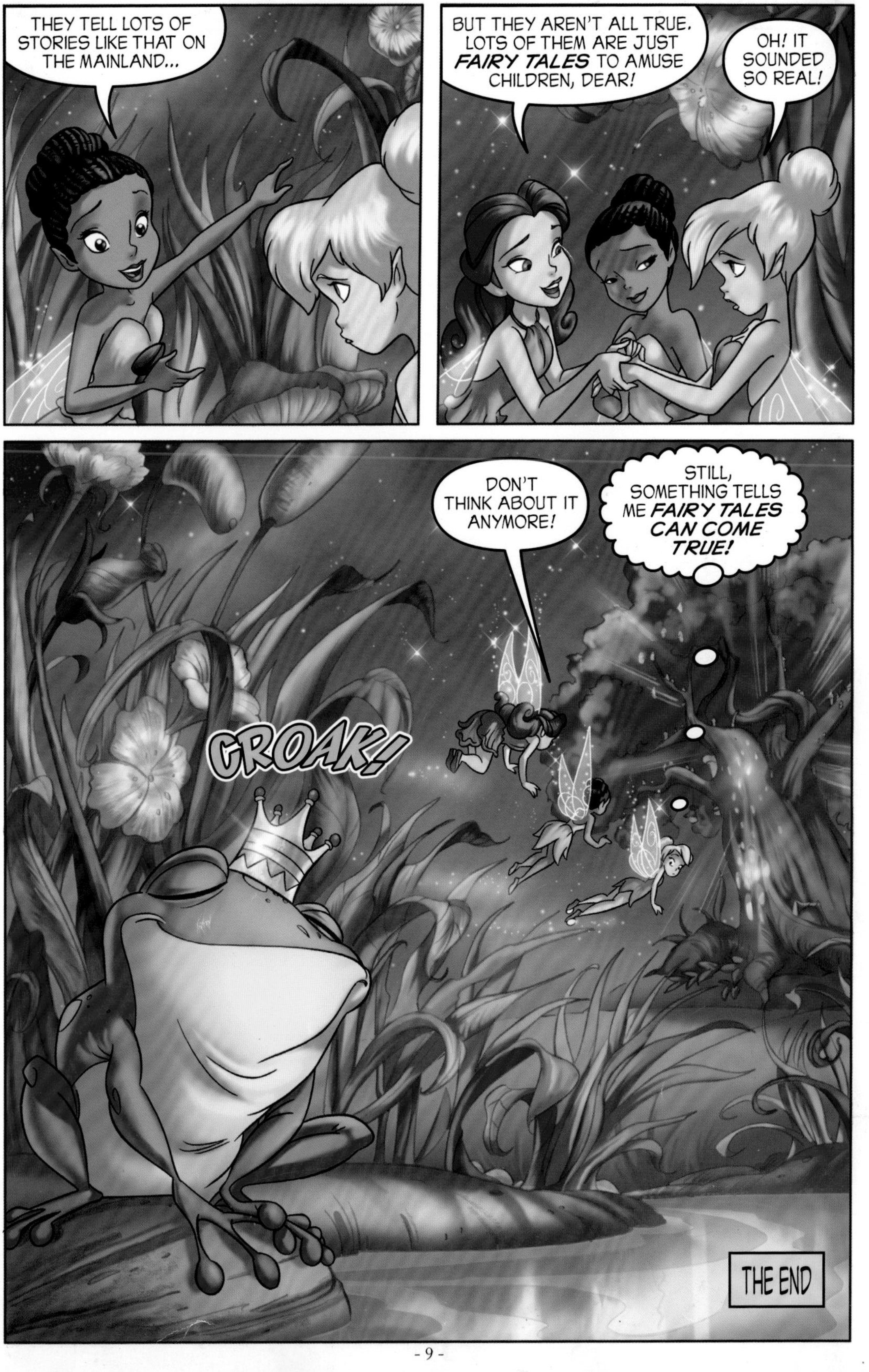
THEY TELL LOTS OF STORIES LIKE THAT ON THE MAINLAND...
BUT THEY AREN'T ALL TRUE. LOTS OF THEM ARE JUST *FAIRY TALES* TO AMUSE CHILDREN, DEAR!
OH! IT SOUNDED SO REAL!
DON'T THINK ABOUT IT ANYMORE!
STILL, SOMETHING TELLS ME *FAIRY TALES CAN COME TRUE!*
CROAK!
THE END

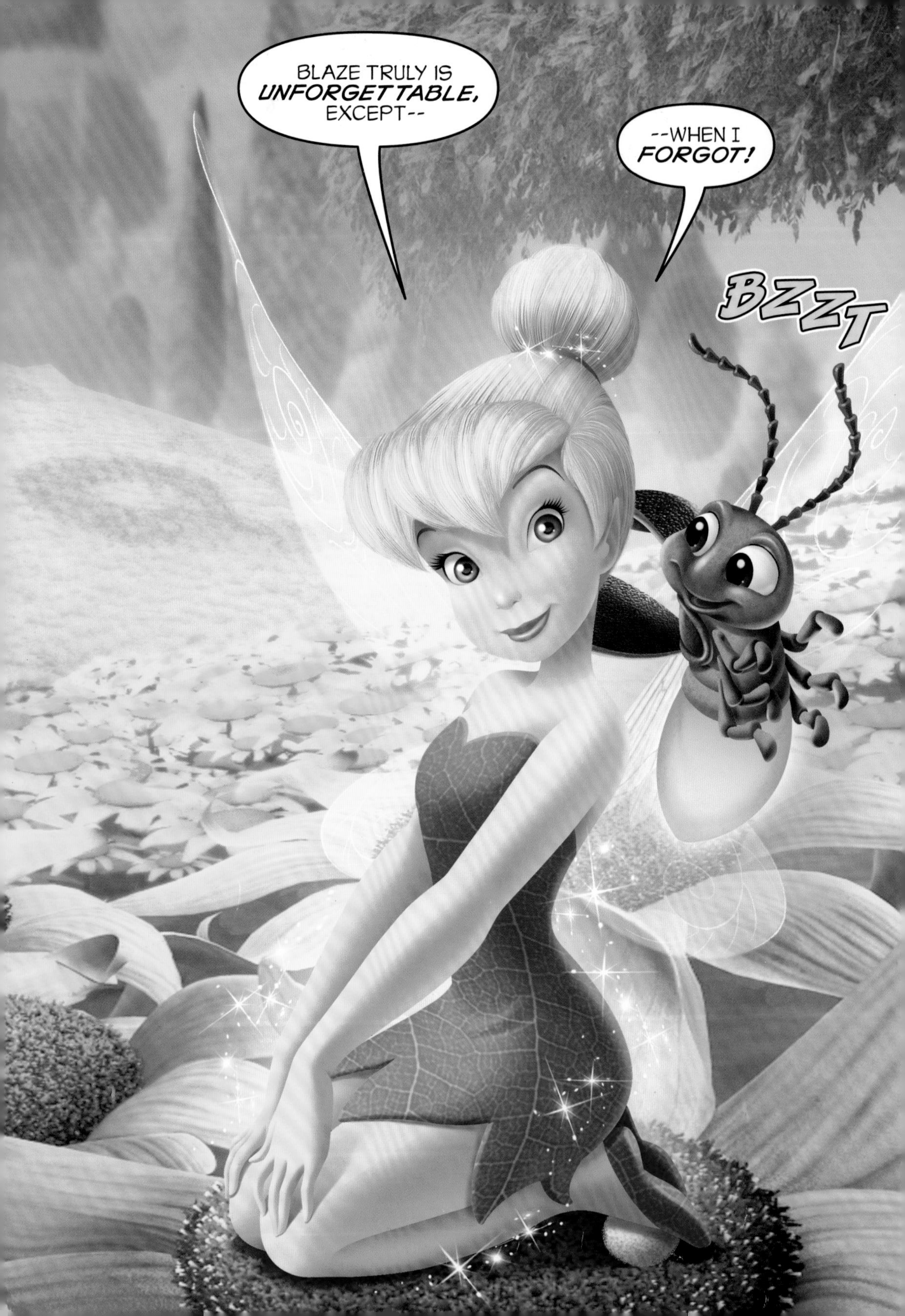
BLAZE TRULY IS *UNFORGETTABLE,* EXCEPT--
--WHEN I *FORGOT!*
BZZT

REMEMBER ME!

BLAZE, LOOK AT ALL THE WONDERFUL LOST OBJECTS I FOUND ON THE SHORE!

I CAN'T WAIT TO START TINKERING WITH SOME OF THIS STUFF!

ISN'T IT *EXCITING?*

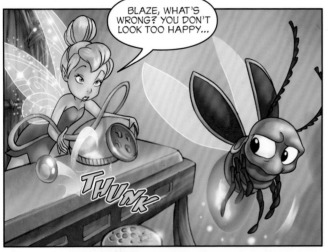

BLAZE, WHAT'S WRONG? YOU DON'T LOOK TOO HAPPY...

THUNK

SLAP

OH, CRACKED KETTLES! I *FORGOT* TO ASK YOU TO GO WITH ME!

I'D FLY BACKWARDS,* BLAZE! NEXT TIME, I'LL *TRY* TO REMEMBER!

* THAT'S HOW FAIRIES SAY "I'M SORRY."

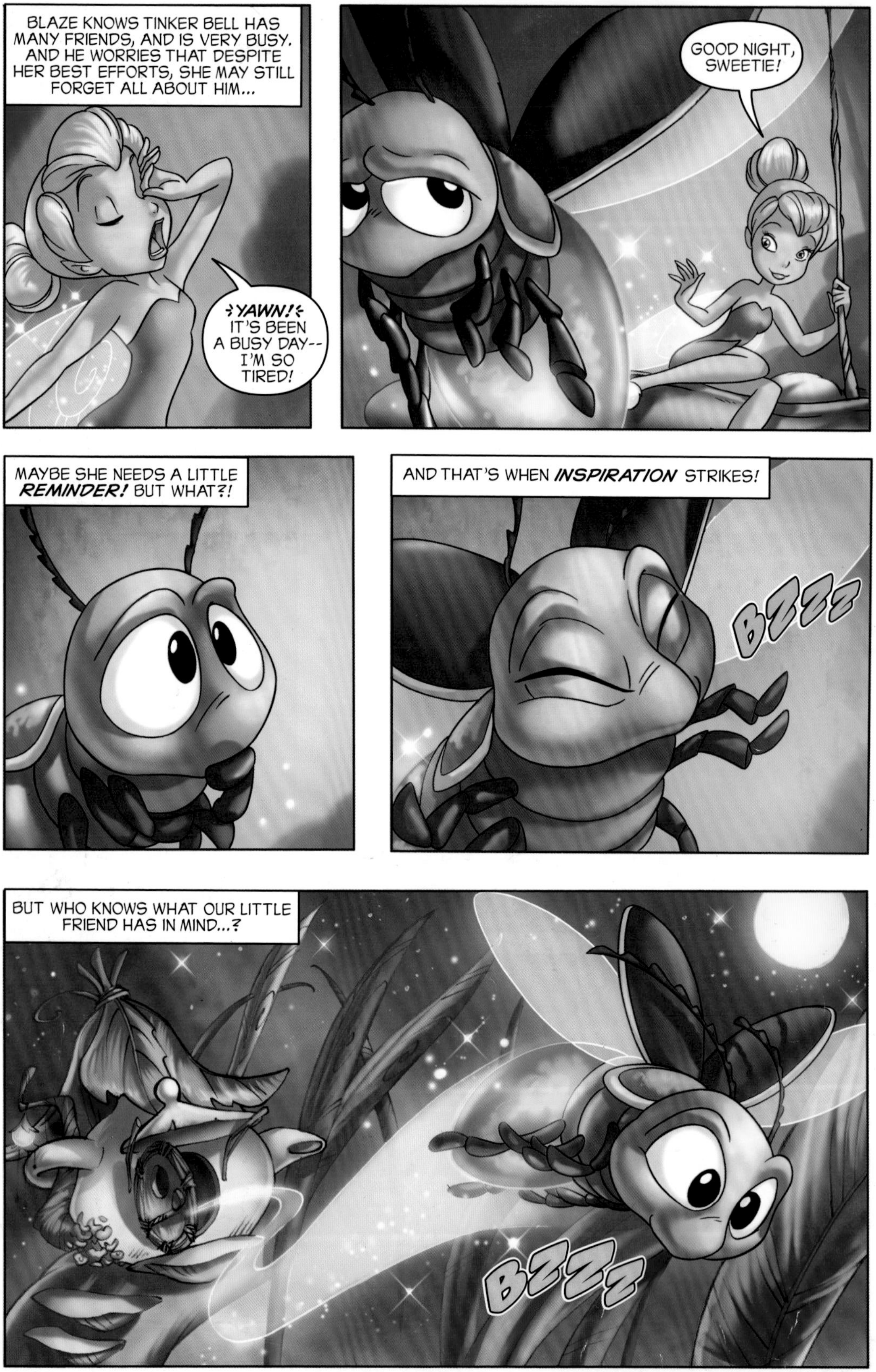
BLAZE KNOWS TINKER BELL HAS MANY FRIENDS, AND IS VERY BUSY. AND HE WORRIES THAT DESPITE HER BEST EFFORTS, SHE MAY STILL FORGET ALL ABOUT HIM...
YAWN! IT'S BEEN A BUSY DAY-- I'M SO TIRED!
GOOD NIGHT, SWEETIE!
MAYBE SHE NEEDS A LITTLE REMINDER! BUT WHAT?!
AND THAT'S WHEN INSPIRATION STRIKES!
BZZZ
BUT WHO KNOWS WHAT OUR LITTLE FRIEND HAS IN MIND...?
BZZZ

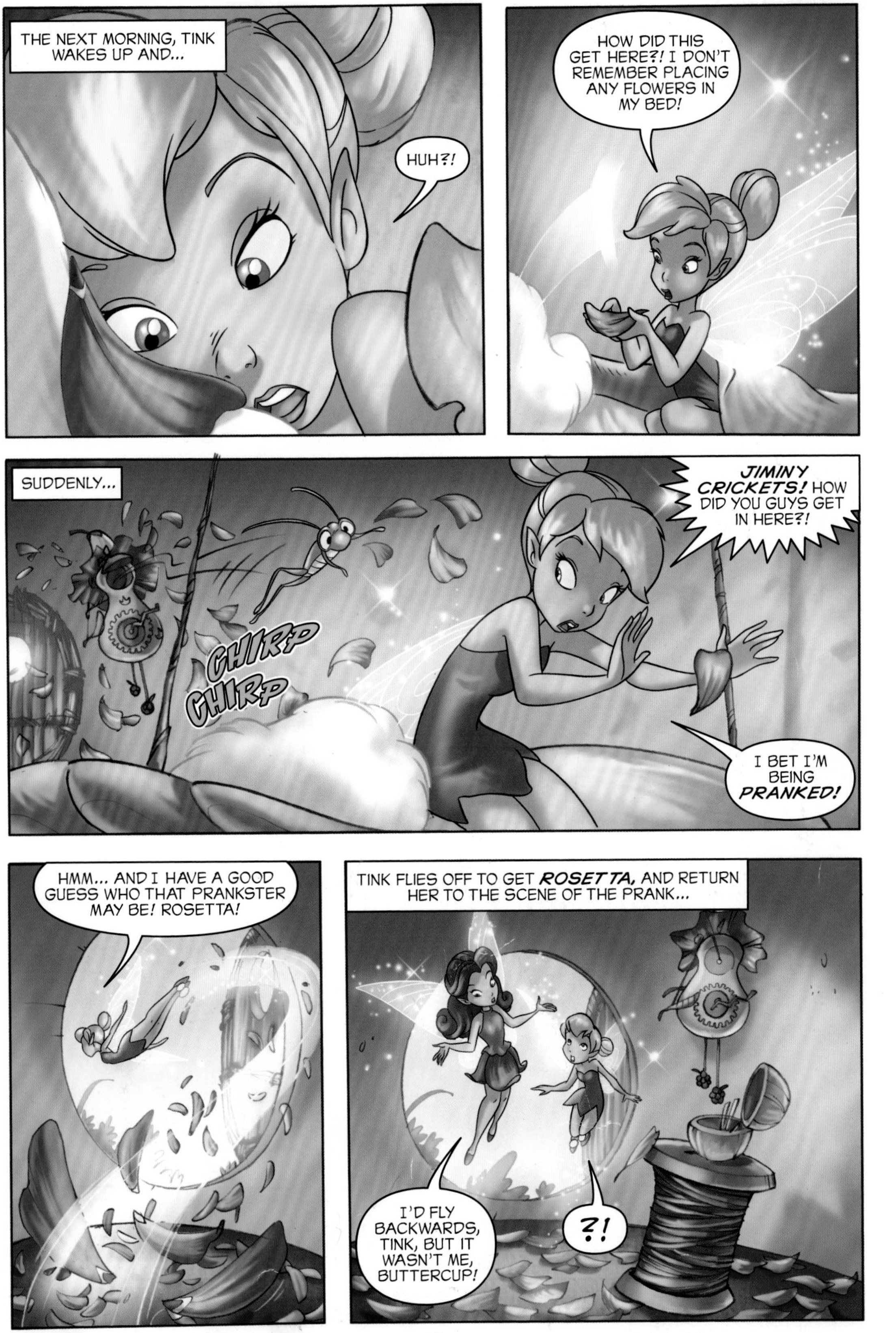
THE NEXT MORNING, TINK WAKES UP AND...
HUH?!
HOW DID THIS GET HERE?! I DON'T REMEMBER PLACING ANY FLOWERS IN MY BED!
SUDDENLY...
CHIRP CHIRP
JIMINY CRICKETS! HOW DID YOU GUYS GET IN HERE?!
I BET I'M BEING PRANKED!
HMM... AND I HAVE A GOOD GUESS WHO THAT PRANKSTER MAY BE! ROSETTA!
TINK FLIES OFF TO GET ROSETTA, AND RETURN HER TO THE SCENE OF THE PRANK...
I'D FLY BACKWARDS, TINK, BUT IT WASN'T ME, BUTTERCUP!
?!

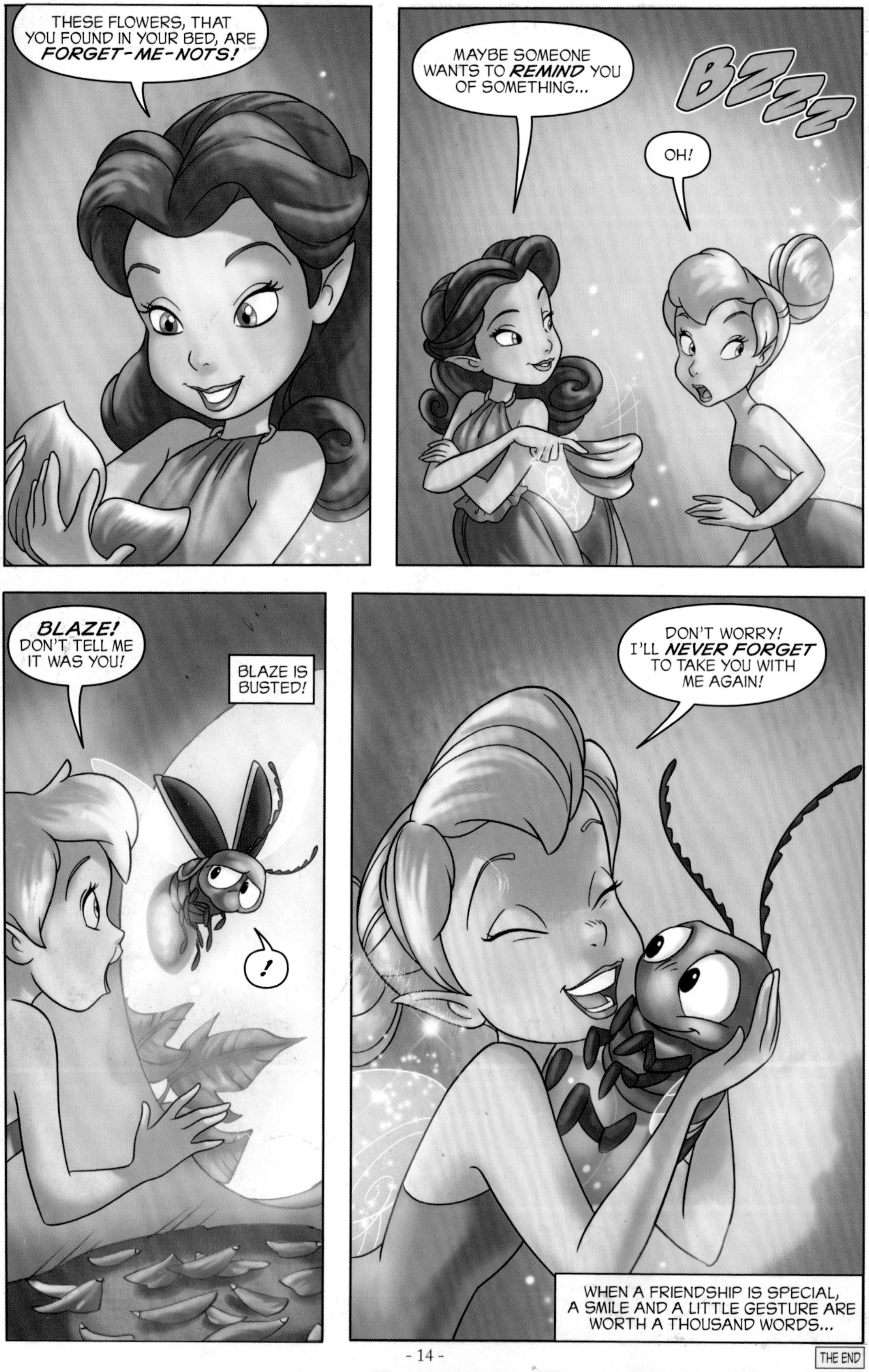
THESE FLOWERS, THAT YOU FOUND IN YOUR BED, ARE FORGET-ME-NOTS!
MAYBE SOMEONE WANTS TO REMIND YOU OF SOMETHING...
BZZZ
OH!
BLAZE! DON'T TELL ME IT WAS YOU!
BLAZE IS BUSTED!
!
DON'T WORRY! I'LL NEVER FORGET TO TAKE YOU WITH ME AGAIN!
WHEN A FRIENDSHIP IS SPECIAL, A SMILE AND A LITTLE GESTURE ARE WORTH A THOUSAND WORDS...

THE END

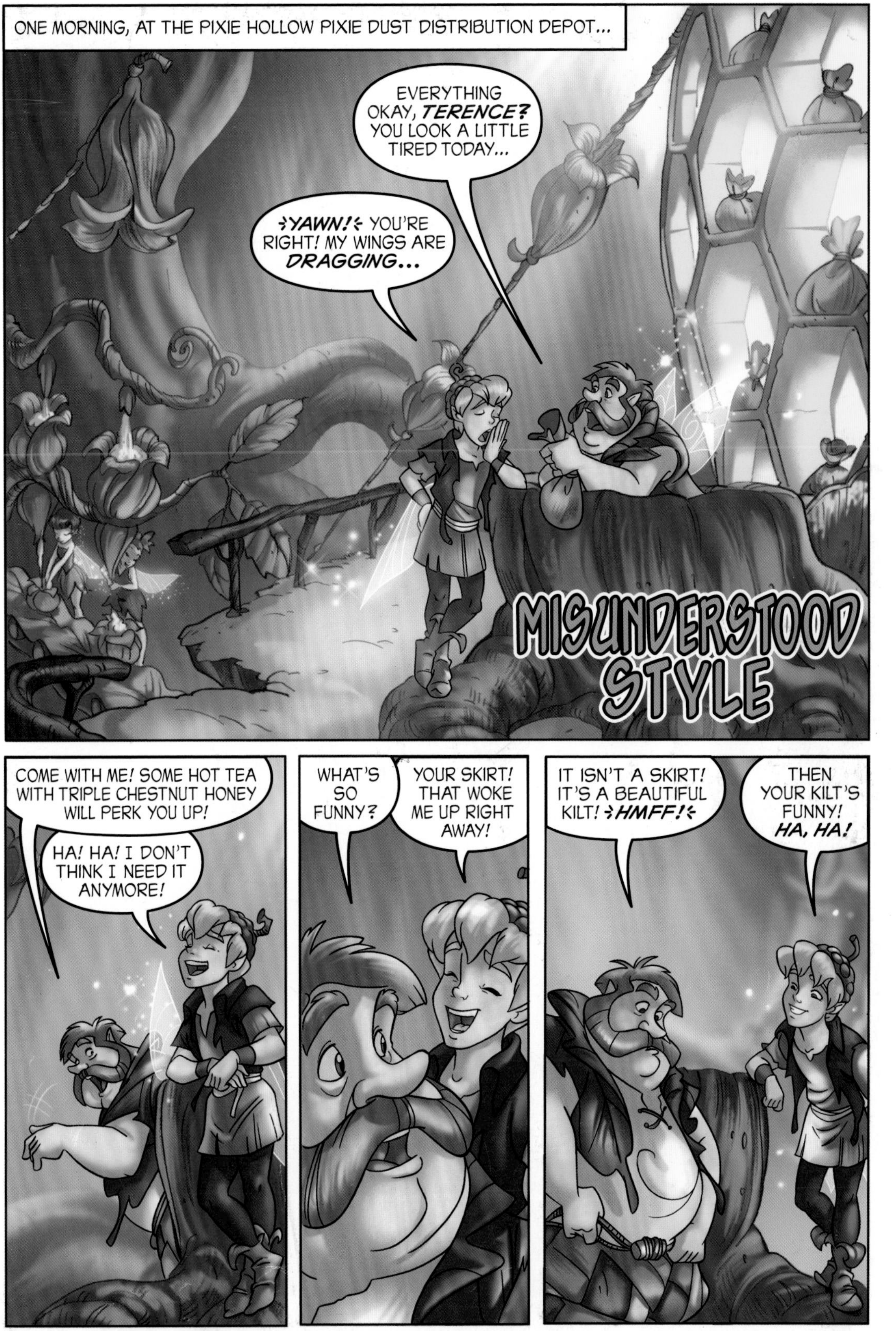

ONE MORNING, AT THE PIXIE HOLLOW PIXIE DUST DISTRIBUTION DEPOT...
EVERYTHING OKAY, TERENCE? YOU LOOK A LITTLE TIRED TODAY...
YAWN! YOU'RE RIGHT! MY WINGS ARE DRAGGING...
MISUNDERSTOOD STYLE
COME WITH ME! SOME HOT TEA WITH TRIPLE CHESTNUT HONEY WILL PERK YOU UP!
HA! HA! I DON'T THINK I NEED IT ANYMORE!
WHAT'S SO FUNNY?
YOUR SKIRT! THAT WOKE ME UP RIGHT AWAY!
IT ISN'T A SKIRT! IT'S A BEAUTIFUL KILT! HMFF!
THEN YOUR KILT'S FUNNY! HA, HA!

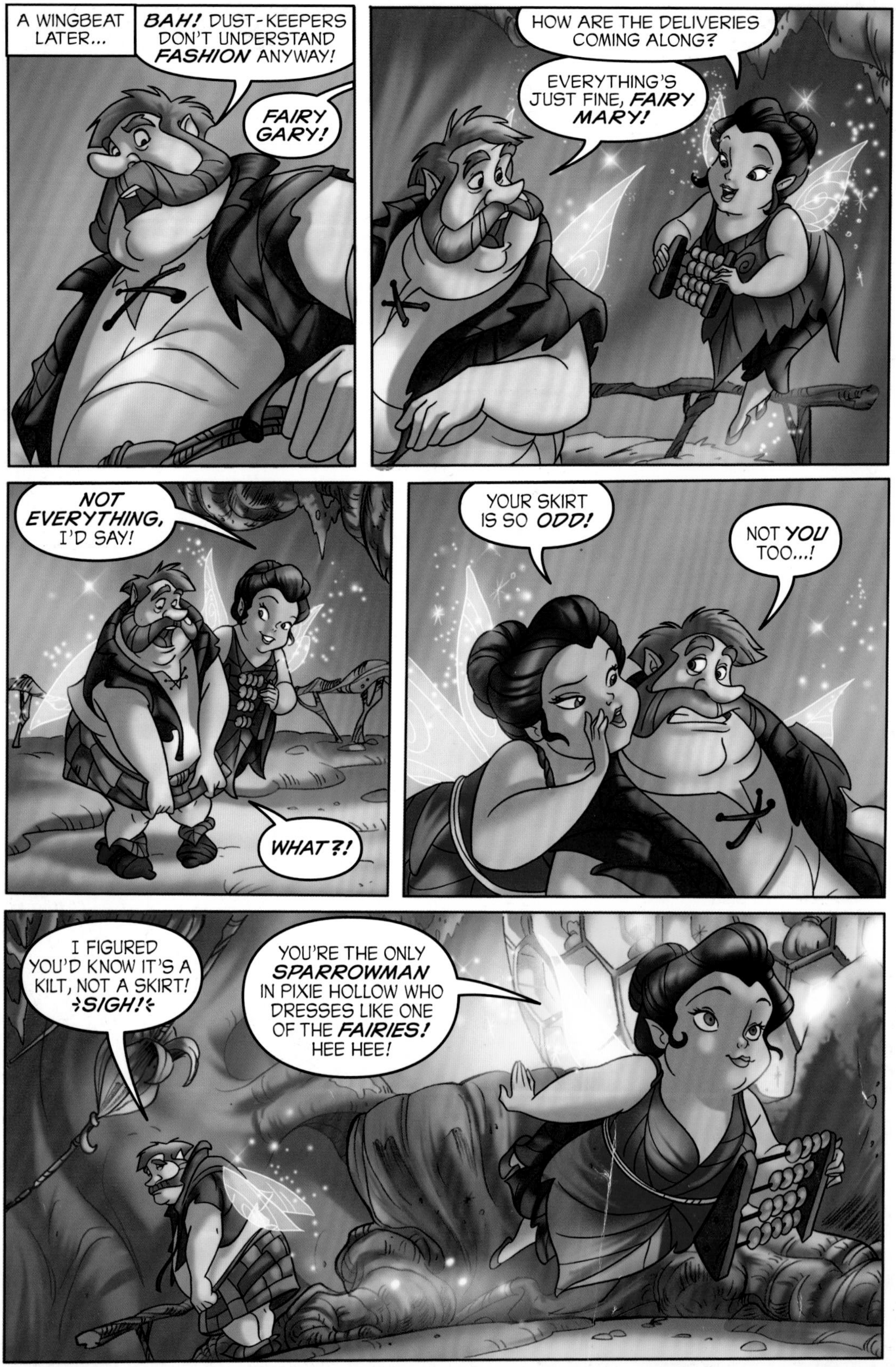
A WINGBEAT LATER...
BAH! DUST-KEEPERS DON'T UNDERSTAND ***FASHION*** ANYWAY!
FAIRY GARY!
HOW ARE THE DELIVERIES COMING ALONG?
EVERYTHING'S JUST FINE, ***FAIRY MARY!***
NOT EVERYTHING, I'D SAY!
WHAT?!
YOUR SKIRT IS SO ***ODD!***
NOT ***YOU*** TOO...!
I FIGURED YOU'D KNOW IT'S A KILT, NOT A SKIRT! ***SIGH!***
YOU'RE THE ONLY ***SPARROWMAN*** IN PIXIE HOLLOW WHO DRESSES LIKE ONE OF THE ***FAIRIES!*** HEE HEE!

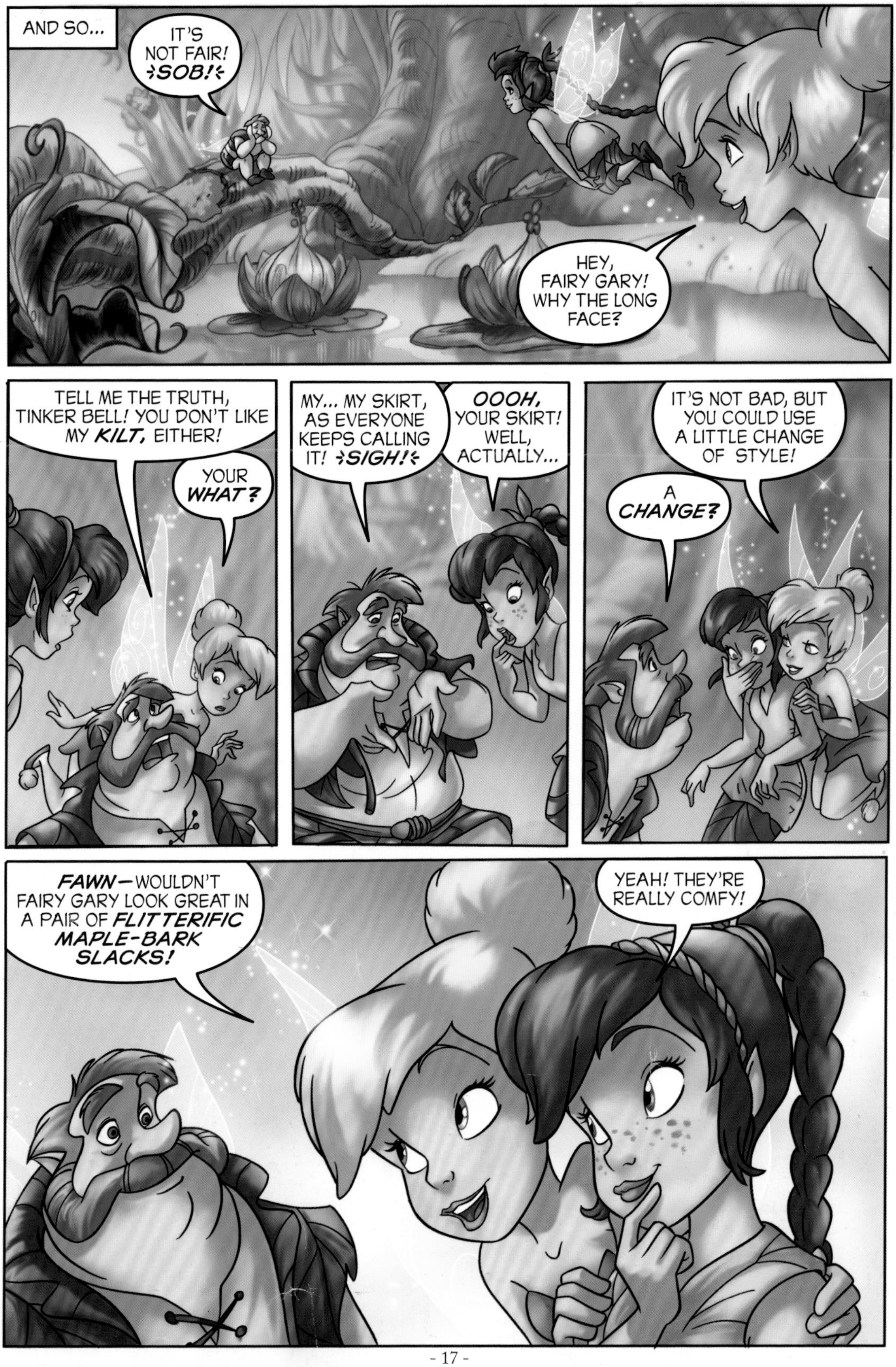
AND SO...
IT'S NOT FAIR! ⊰SOB!⊱
HEY, FAIRY GARY! WHY THE LONG FACE?
TELL ME THE TRUTH, TINKER BELL! YOU DON'T LIKE MY KILT, EITHER!
YOUR WHAT?
MY... MY SKIRT, AS EVERYONE KEEPS CALLING IT! ⊰SIGH!⊱
OOOH, YOUR SKIRT! WELL, ACTUALLY...
IT'S NOT BAD, BUT YOU COULD USE A LITTLE CHANGE OF STYLE!
A CHANGE?
FAWN—WOULDN'T FAIRY GARY LOOK GREAT IN A PAIR OF FLITTERIFIC MAPLE-BARK SLACKS!
YEAH! THEY'RE REALLY COMFY!

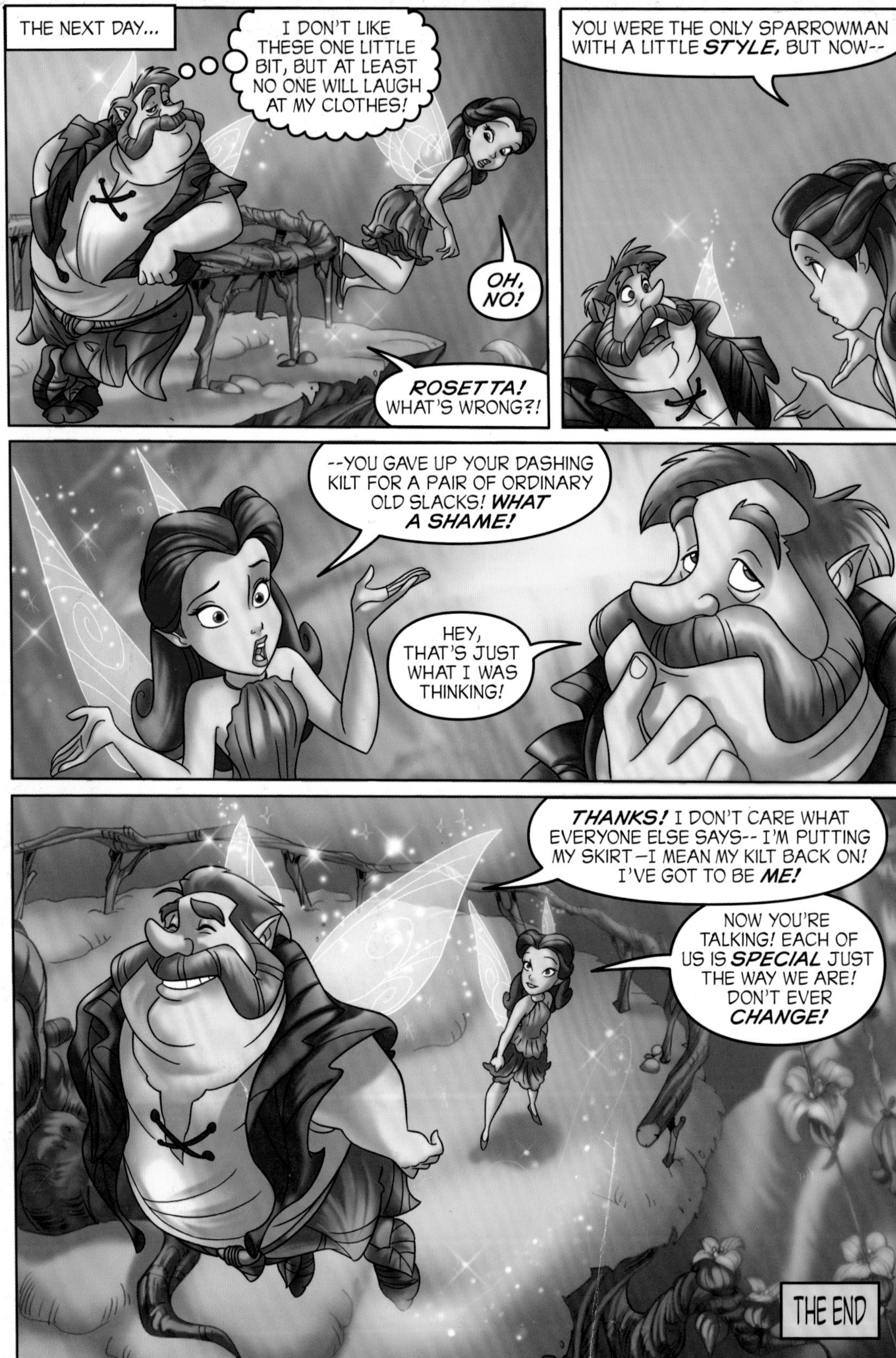
THE NEXT DAY...
I DON'T LIKE THESE ONE LITTLE BIT, BUT AT LEAST NO ONE WILL LAUGH AT MY CLOTHES!
OH, NO!
ROSETTA! WHAT'S WRONG?!
YOU WERE THE ONLY SPARROWMAN WITH A LITTLE STYLE, BUT NOW--
--YOU GAVE UP YOUR DASHING KILT FOR A PAIR OF ORDINARY OLD SLACKS! WHAT A SHAME!
HEY, THAT'S JUST WHAT I WAS THINKING!
THANKS! I DON'T CARE WHAT EVERYONE ELSE SAYS-- I'M PUTTING MY SKIRT—I MEAN MY KILT BACK ON! I'VE GOT TO BE ME!
NOW YOU'RE TALKING! EACH OF US IS SPECIAL JUST THE WAY WE ARE! DON'T EVER CHANGE!
THE END

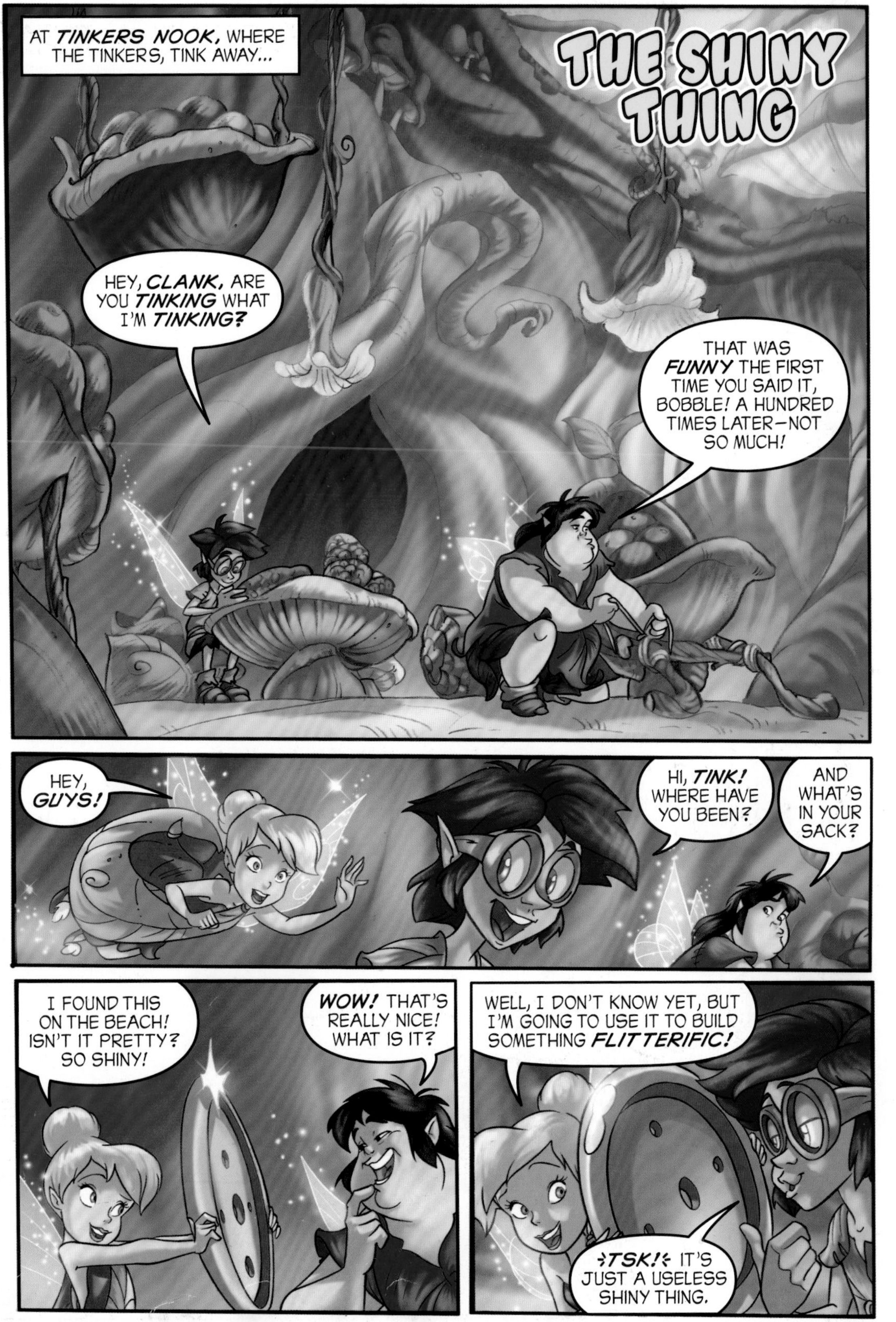
AT TINKERS NOOK, WHERE THE TINKERS, TINK AWAY...
THE SHINY THING
HEY, CLANK, ARE YOU TINKING WHAT I'M TINKING?
THAT WAS FUNNY THE FIRST TIME YOU SAID IT, BOBBLE! A HUNDRED TIMES LATER—NOT SO MUCH!
HEY, GUYS!
HI, TINK! WHERE HAVE YOU BEEN?
AND WHAT'S IN YOUR SACK?
I FOUND THIS ON THE BEACH! ISN'T IT PRETTY? SO SHINY!
WOW! THAT'S REALLY NICE! WHAT IS IT?
WELL, I DON'T KNOW YET, BUT I'M GOING TO USE IT TO BUILD SOMETHING FLITTERIFIC!
TSK! IT'S JUST A USELESS SHINY THING.

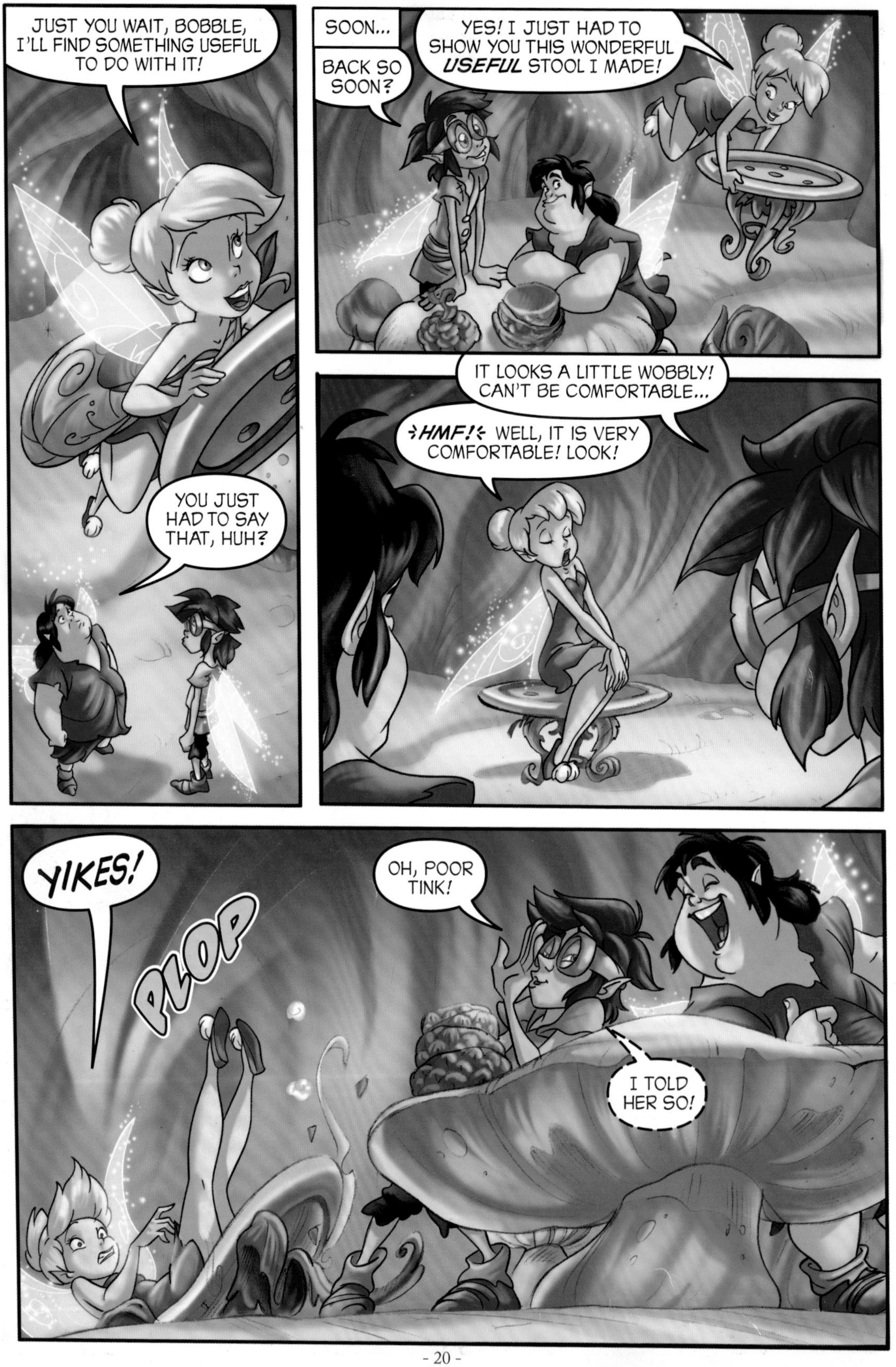
JUST YOU WAIT, BOBBLE, I'LL FIND SOMETHING USEFUL TO DO WITH IT!
YOU JUST HAD TO SAY THAT, HUH?
SOON...
BACK SO SOON?
YES! I JUST HAD TO SHOW YOU THIS WONDERFUL USEFUL STOOL I MADE!
IT LOOKS A LITTLE WOBBLY! CAN'T BE COMFORTABLE...
HMF! WELL, IT IS VERY COMFORTABLE! LOOK!
YIKES!
PLOP
OH, POOR TINK!
I TOLD HER SO!

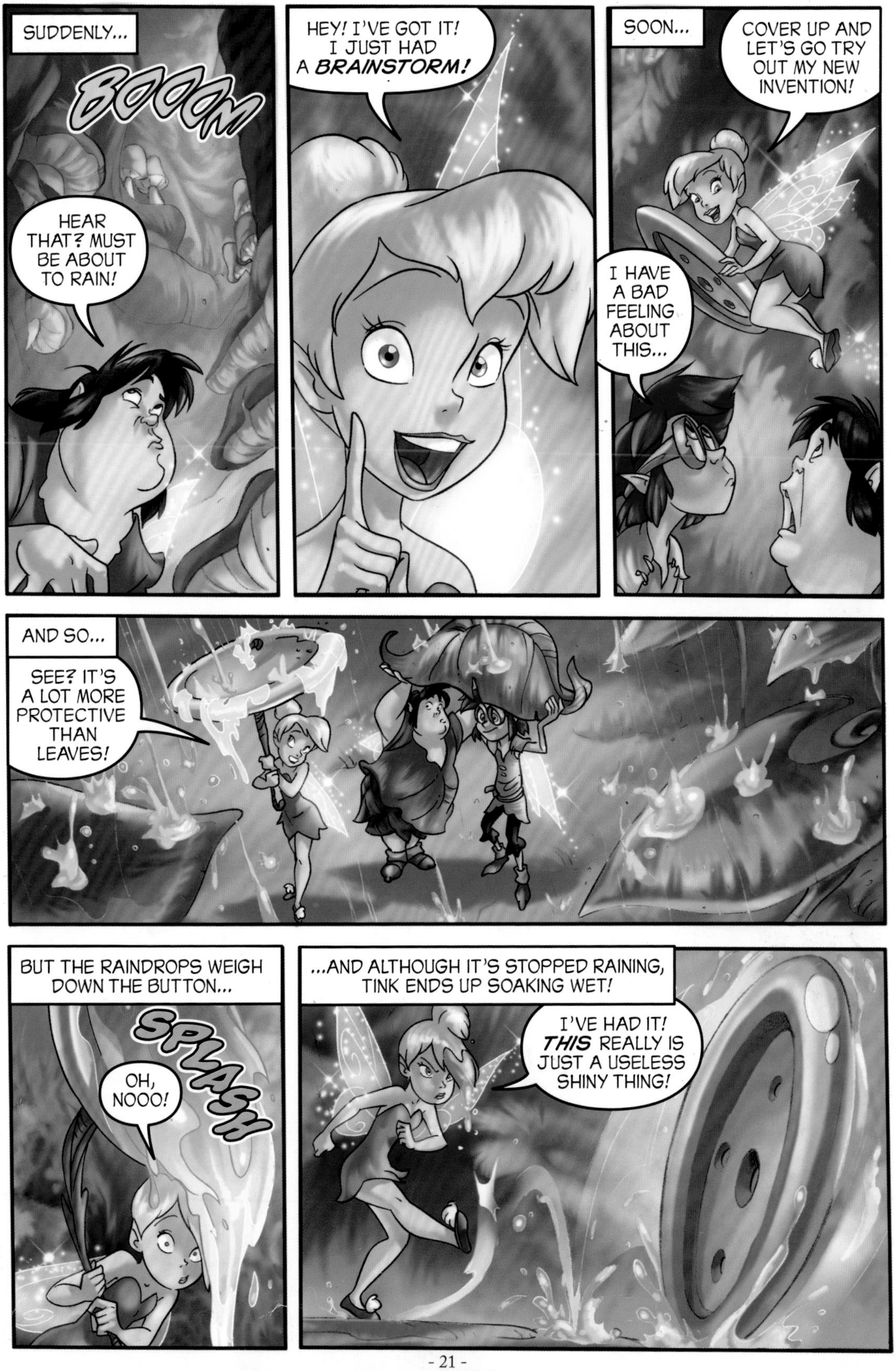
SUDDENLY...
BOOOM
HEAR THAT? MUST BE ABOUT TO RAIN!
HEY! I'VE GOT IT! I JUST HAD A BRAINSTORM!
SOON...
COVER UP AND LET'S GO TRY OUT MY NEW INVENTION!
I HAVE A BAD FEELING ABOUT THIS...
AND SO...
SEE? IT'S A LOT MORE PROTECTIVE THAN LEAVES!
BUT THE RAINDROPS WEIGH DOWN THE BUTTON...
SPLASH
OH, NOOO!
...AND ALTHOUGH IT'S STOPPED RAINING, TINK ENDS UP SOAKING WET!
I'VE HAD IT! THIS REALLY IS JUST A USELESS SHINY THING!

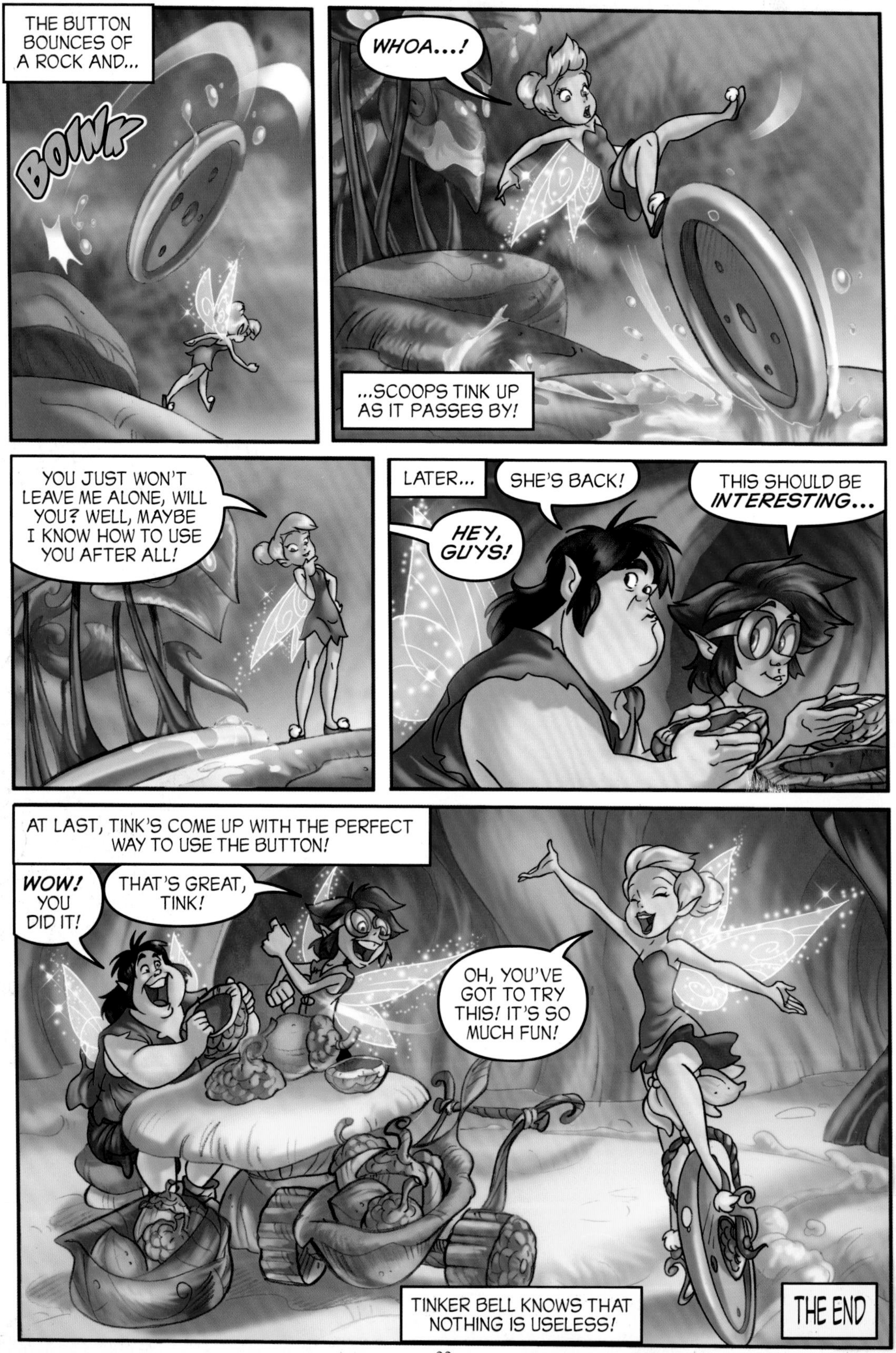
THE BUTTON BOUNCES OF A ROCK AND...
BOINK
WHOA...!
...SCOOPS TINK UP AS IT PASSES BY!
YOU JUST WON'T LEAVE ME ALONE, WILL YOU? WELL, MAYBE I KNOW HOW TO USE YOU AFTER ALL!
LATER...
SHE'S BACK!
THIS SHOULD BE *INTERESTING...*
HEY, GUYS!
AT LAST, TINK'S COME UP WITH THE PERFECT WAY TO USE THE BUTTON!
WOW! YOU DID IT!
THAT'S GREAT, TINK!
OH, YOU'VE GOT TO TRY THIS! IT'S SO MUCH FUN!
TINKER BELL KNOWS THAT NOTHING IS USELESS!
THE END

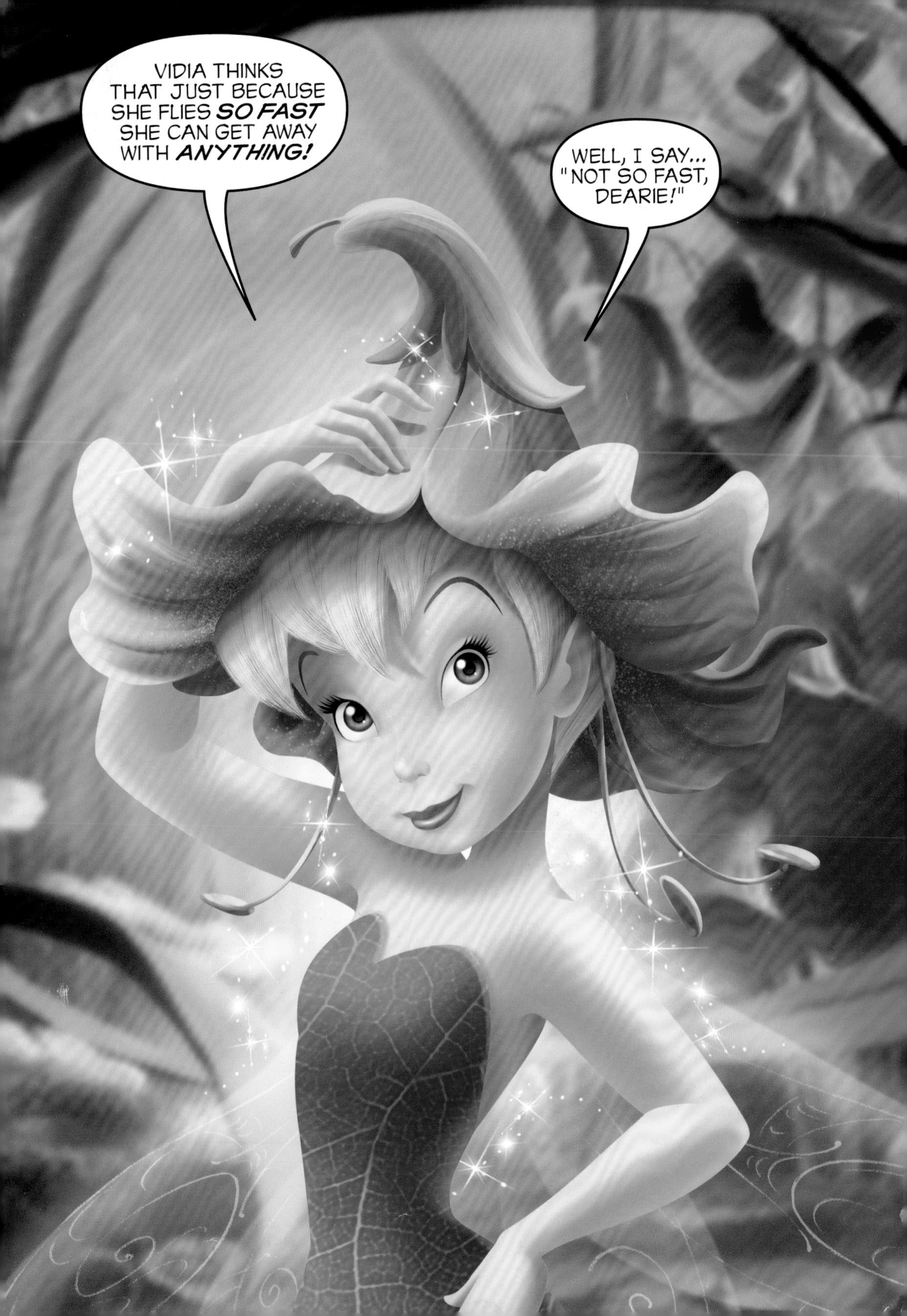
VIDIA THINKS THAT JUST BECAUSE SHE FLIES SO FAST SHE CAN GET AWAY WITH ANYTHING!
WELL, I SAY... "NOT SO FAST, DEARIE!"

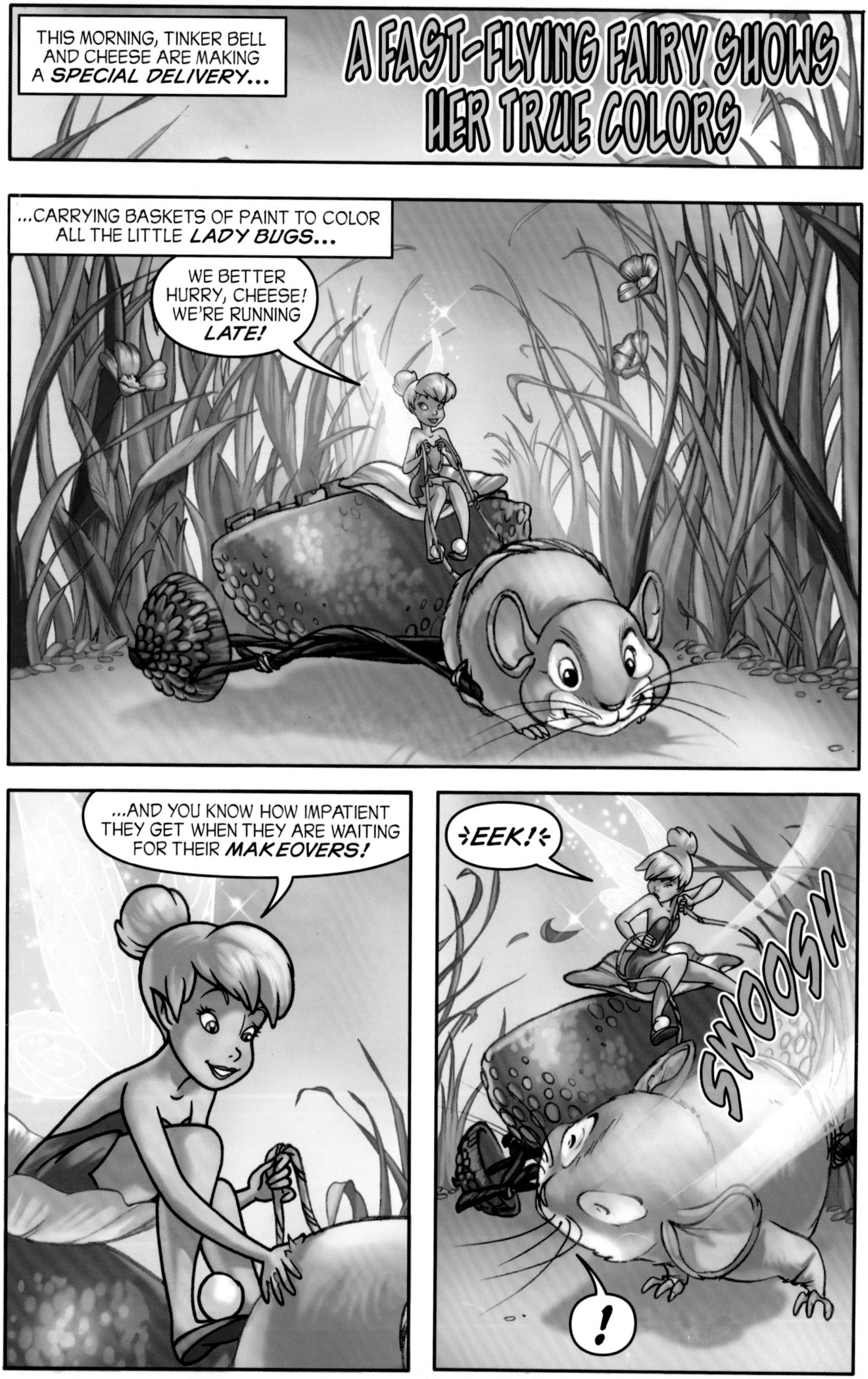
THIS MORNING, TINKER BELL AND CHEESE ARE MAKING A SPECIAL DELIVERY...
A FAST-FLYING FAIRY SHOWS HER TRUE COLORS
...CARRYING BASKETS OF PAINT TO COLOR ALL THE LITTLE LADY BUGS...
WE BETTER HURRY, CHEESE! WE'RE RUNNING LATE!
...AND YOU KNOW HOW IMPATIENT THEY GET WHEN THEY ARE WAITING FOR THEIR MAKEOVERS!
EEK!
SWOOSH
!

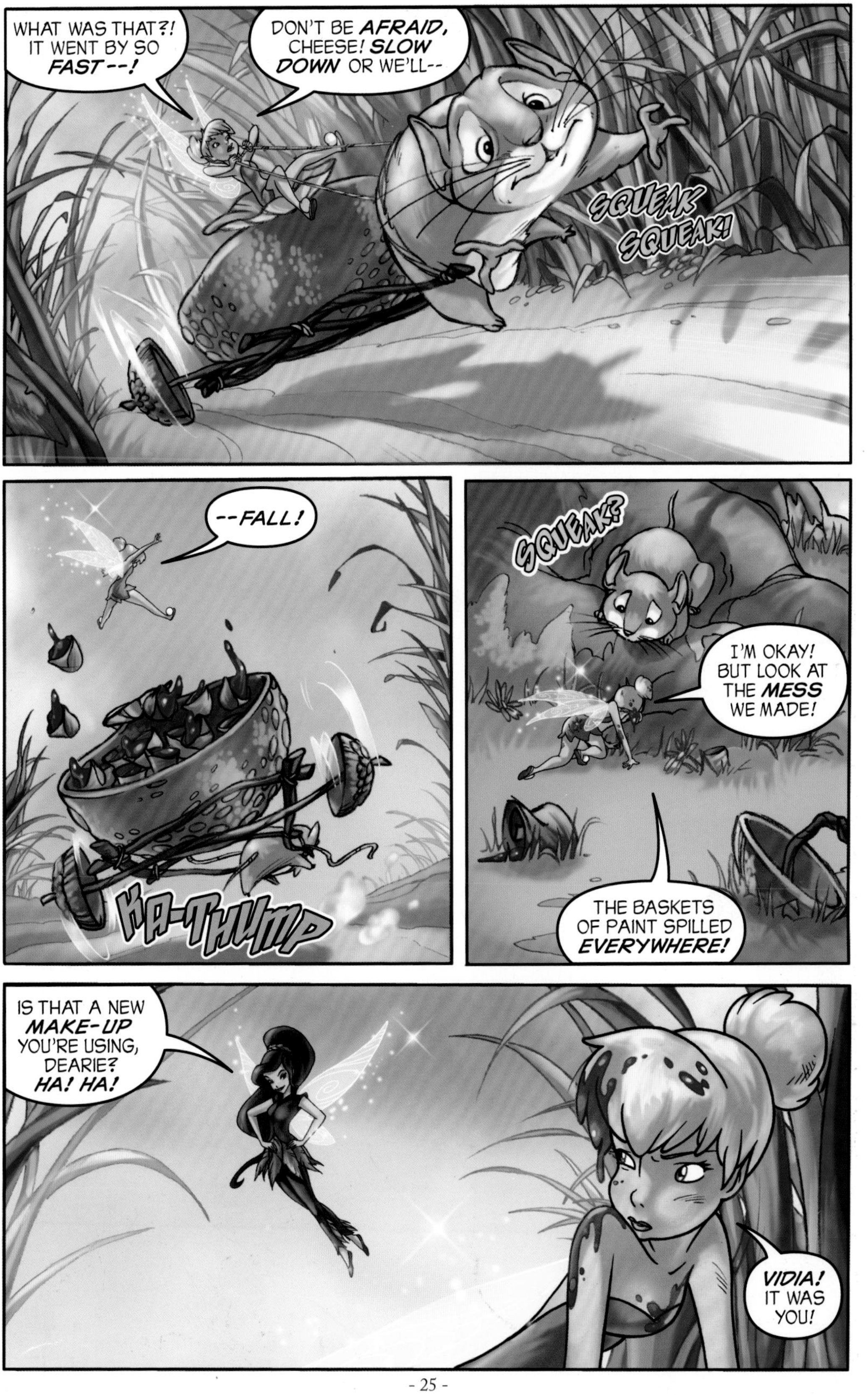
WHAT WAS THAT?! IT WENT BY SO FAST--!
DON'T BE AFRAID, CHEESE! SLOW DOWN OR WE'LL--
SQUEAK SQUEAK!
--FALL!
KA-THUMP
SQUEAK?
I'M OKAY! BUT LOOK AT THE MESS WE MADE!
THE BASKETS OF PAINT SPILLED EVERYWHERE!
IS THAT A NEW MAKE-UP YOU'RE USING, DEARIE? HA! HA!
VIDIA! IT WAS YOU!

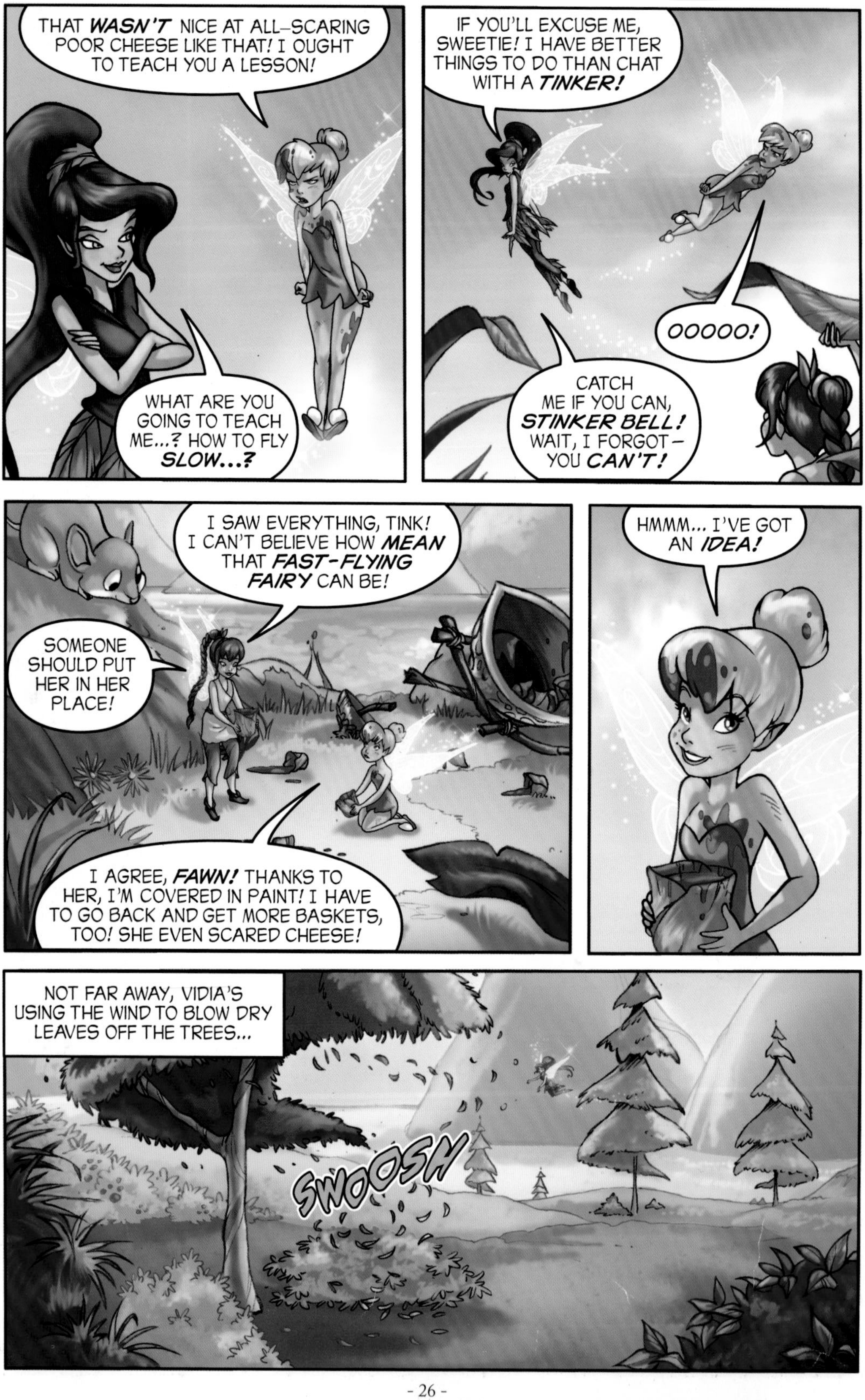

THAT WASN'T NICE AT ALL—SCARING POOR CHEESE LIKE THAT! I OUGHT TO TEACH YOU A LESSON!
WHAT ARE YOU GOING TO TEACH ME...? HOW TO FLY SLOW...?
IF YOU'LL EXCUSE ME, SWEETIE! I HAVE BETTER THINGS TO DO THAN CHAT WITH A TINKER!
OOOOO!
CATCH ME IF YOU CAN, STINKER BELL! WAIT, I FORGOT—YOU CAN'T!
I SAW EVERYTHING, TINK! I CAN'T BELIEVE HOW MEAN THAT FAST-FLYING FAIRY CAN BE!
SOMEONE SHOULD PUT HER IN HER PLACE!
I AGREE, FAWN! THANKS TO HER, I'M COVERED IN PAINT! I HAVE TO GO BACK AND GET MORE BASKETS, TOO! SHE EVEN SCARED CHEESE!
HMMM... I'VE GOT AN IDEA!
NOT FAR AWAY, VIDIA'S USING THE WIND TO BLOW DRY LEAVES OFF THE TREES...
SWOOSH

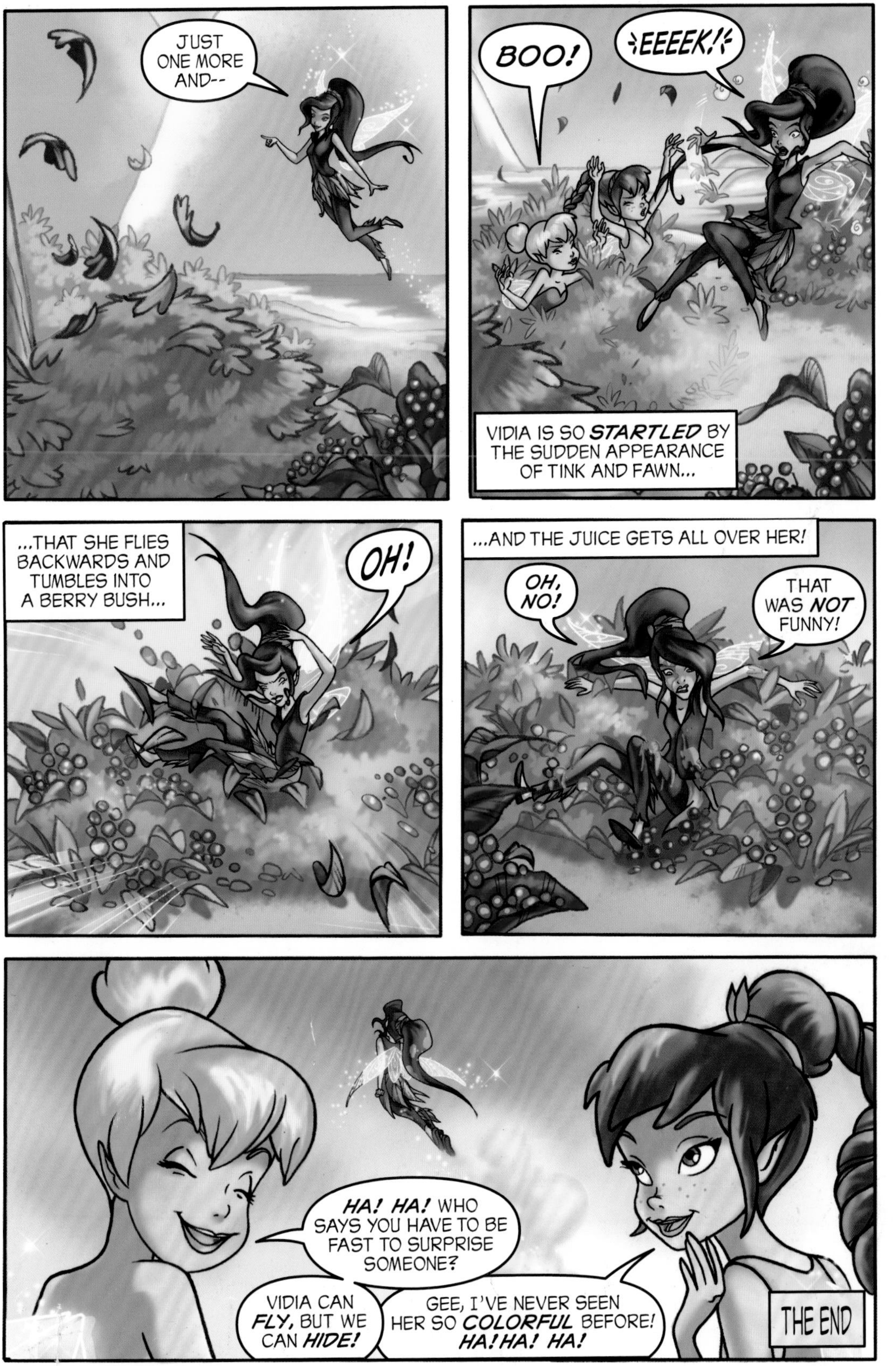
JUST ONE MORE AND--
BOO!
EEEEK!
VIDIA IS SO STARTLED BY THE SUDDEN APPEARANCE OF TINK AND FAWN...
...THAT SHE FLIES BACKWARDS AND TUMBLES INTO A BERRY BUSH...
OH!
...AND THE JUICE GETS ALL OVER HER!
OH, NO!
THAT WAS NOT FUNNY!
HA! HA! WHO SAYS YOU HAVE TO BE FAST TO SURPRISE SOMEONE?
VIDIA CAN FLY, BUT WE CAN HIDE!
GEE, I'VE NEVER SEEN HER SO COLORFUL BEFORE! HA! HA! HA!
THE END

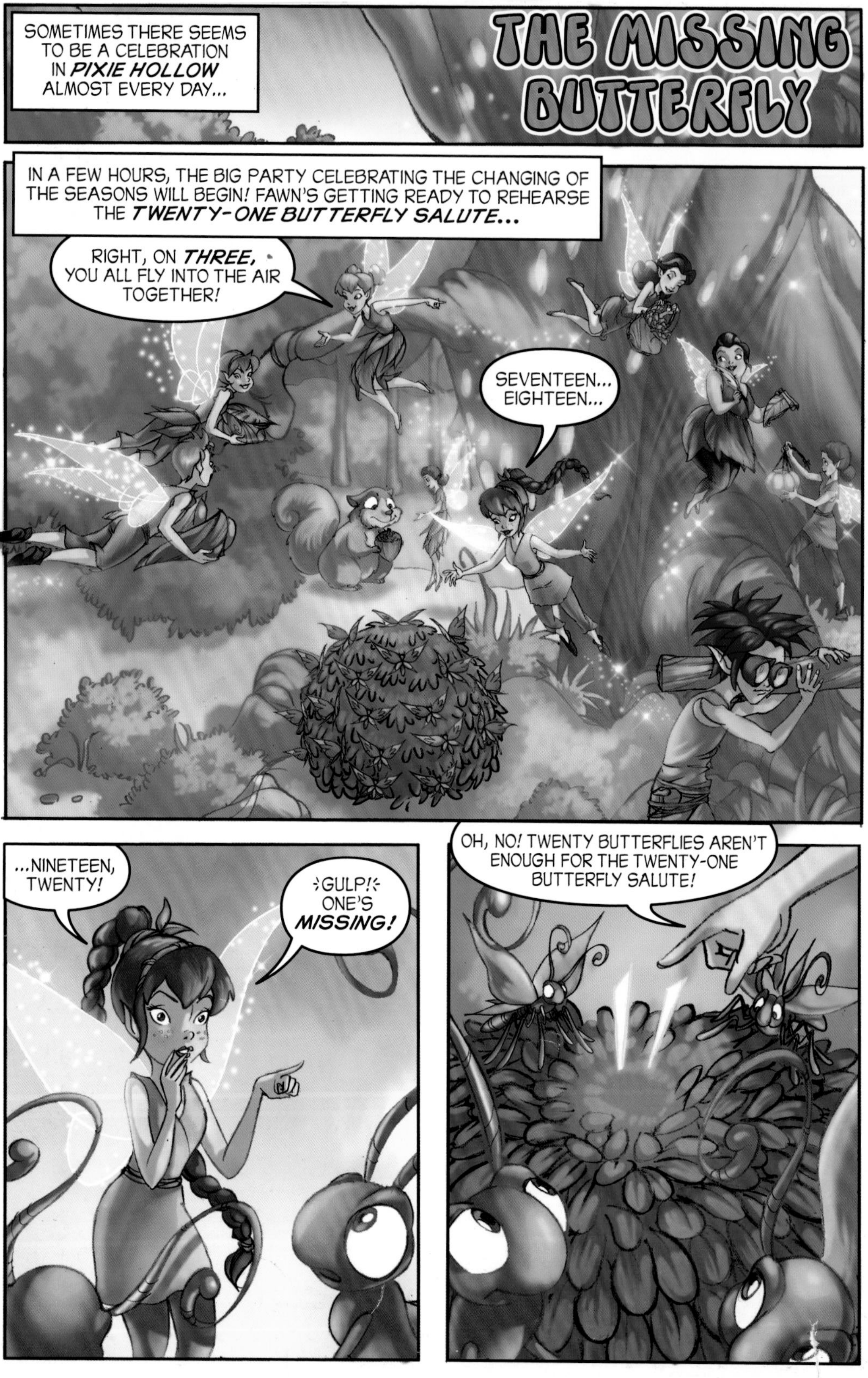
SOMETIMES THERE SEEMS TO BE A CELEBRATION IN *PIXIE HOLLOW* ALMOST EVERY DAY...
THE MISSING BUTTERFLY
IN A FEW HOURS, THE BIG PARTY CELEBRATING THE CHANGING OF THE SEASONS WILL BEGIN! FAWN'S GETTING READY TO REHEARSE THE *TWENTY-ONE BUTTERFLY SALUTE...*
RIGHT, ON *THREE,* YOU ALL FLY INTO THE AIR TOGETHER!
SEVENTEEN... EIGHTEEN...
...NINETEEN, TWENTY!
GULP! ONE'S *MISSING!*
OH, NO! TWENTY BUTTERFLIES AREN'T ENOUGH FOR THE TWENTY-ONE BUTTERFLY SALUTE!

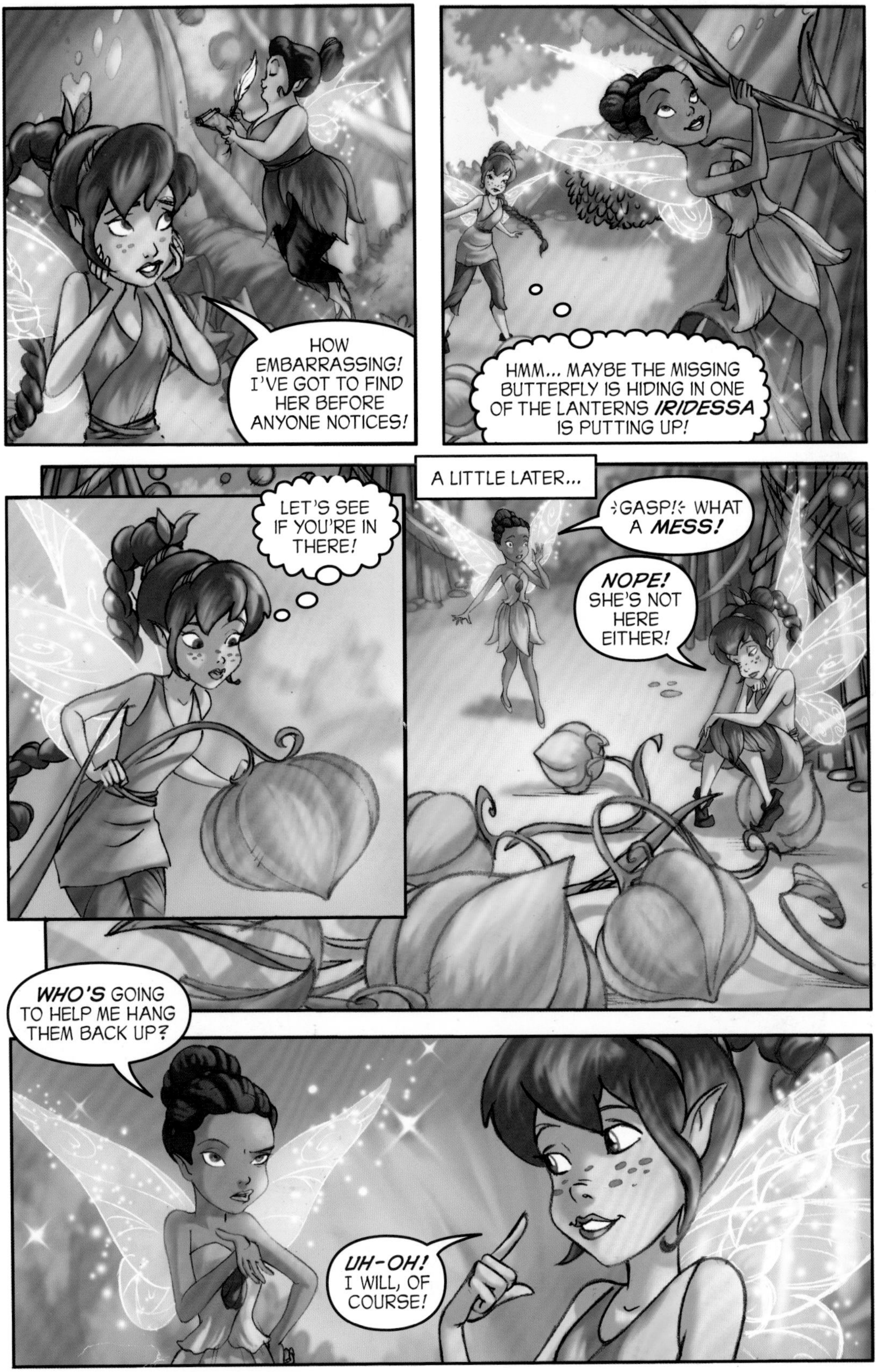
HOW EMBARRASSING! I'VE GOT TO FIND HER BEFORE ANYONE NOTICES!
HMM... MAYBE THE MISSING BUTTERFLY IS HIDING IN ONE OF THE LANTERNS *IRIDESSA* IS PUTTING UP!
A LITTLE LATER...
LET'S SEE IF YOU'RE IN THERE!
GASP! WHAT A ***MESS!***
NOPE! SHE'S NOT HERE EITHER!
WHO'S GOING TO HELP ME HANG THEM BACK UP?
UH-OH! I WILL, OF COURSE!

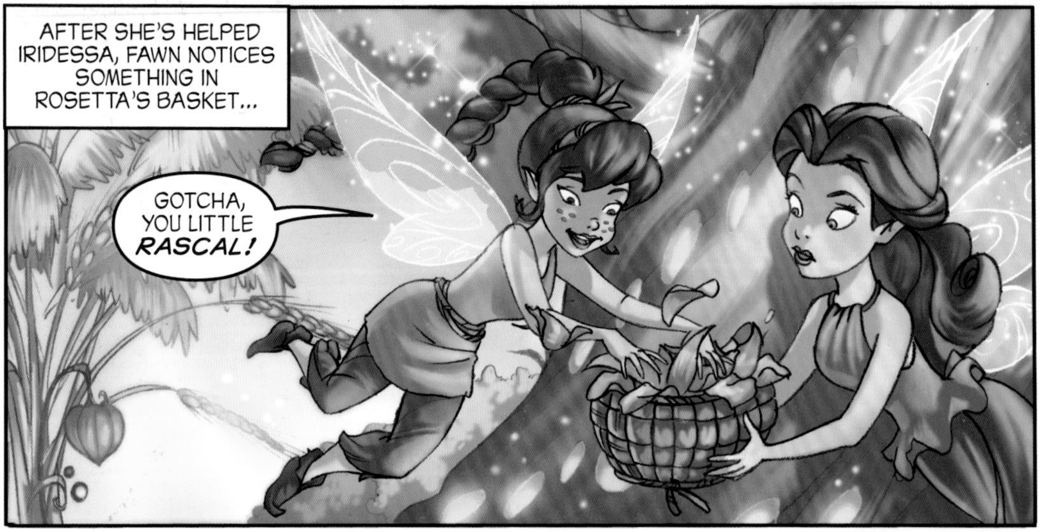
AFTER SHE'S HELPED IRIDESSA, FAWN NOTICES SOMETHING IN ROSETTA'S BASKET...
GOTCHA, YOU LITTLE RASCAL!

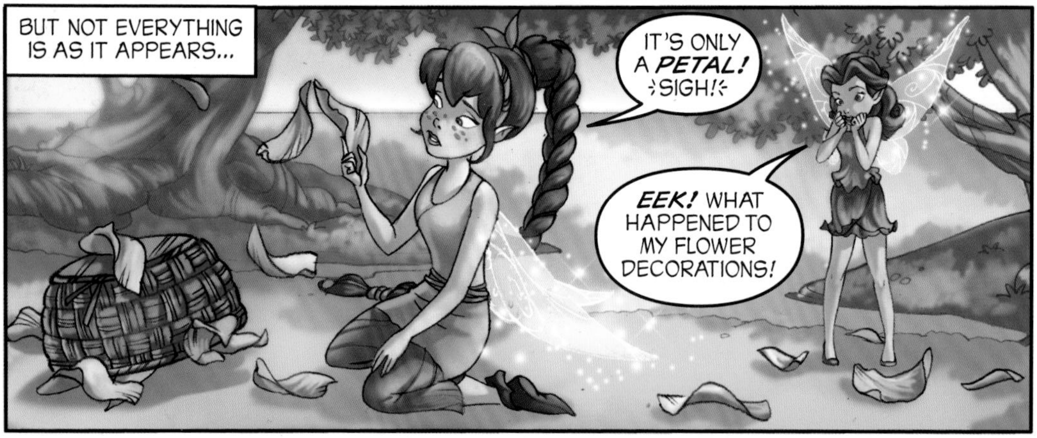
BUT NOT EVERYTHING IS AS IT APPEARS...
IT'S ONLY A PETAL! ⊰SIGH!⊱
EEK! WHAT HAPPENED TO MY FLOWER DECORATIONS!

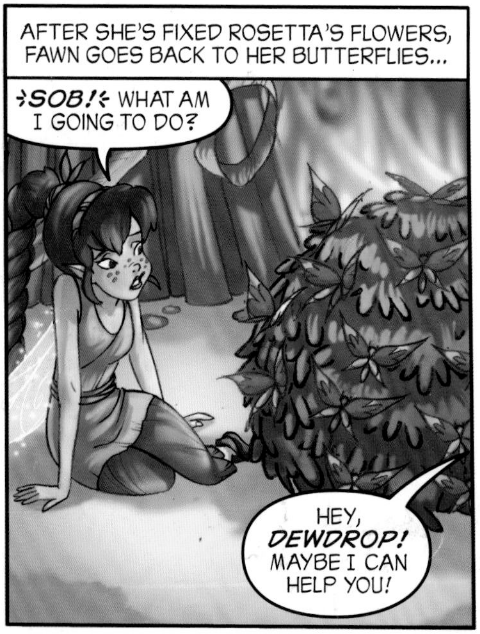
AFTER SHE'S FIXED ROSETTA'S FLOWERS, FAWN GOES BACK TO HER BUTTERFLIES...
⊰SOB!⊱ WHAT AM I GOING TO DO?
HEY, DEWDROP! MAYBE I CAN HELP YOU!

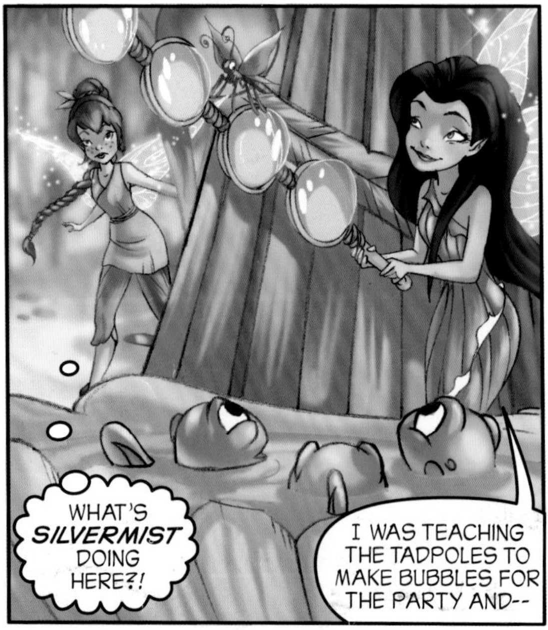
WHAT'S SILVERMIST DOING HERE?!
I WAS TEACHING THE TADPOLES TO MAKE BUBBLES FOR THE PARTY AND--

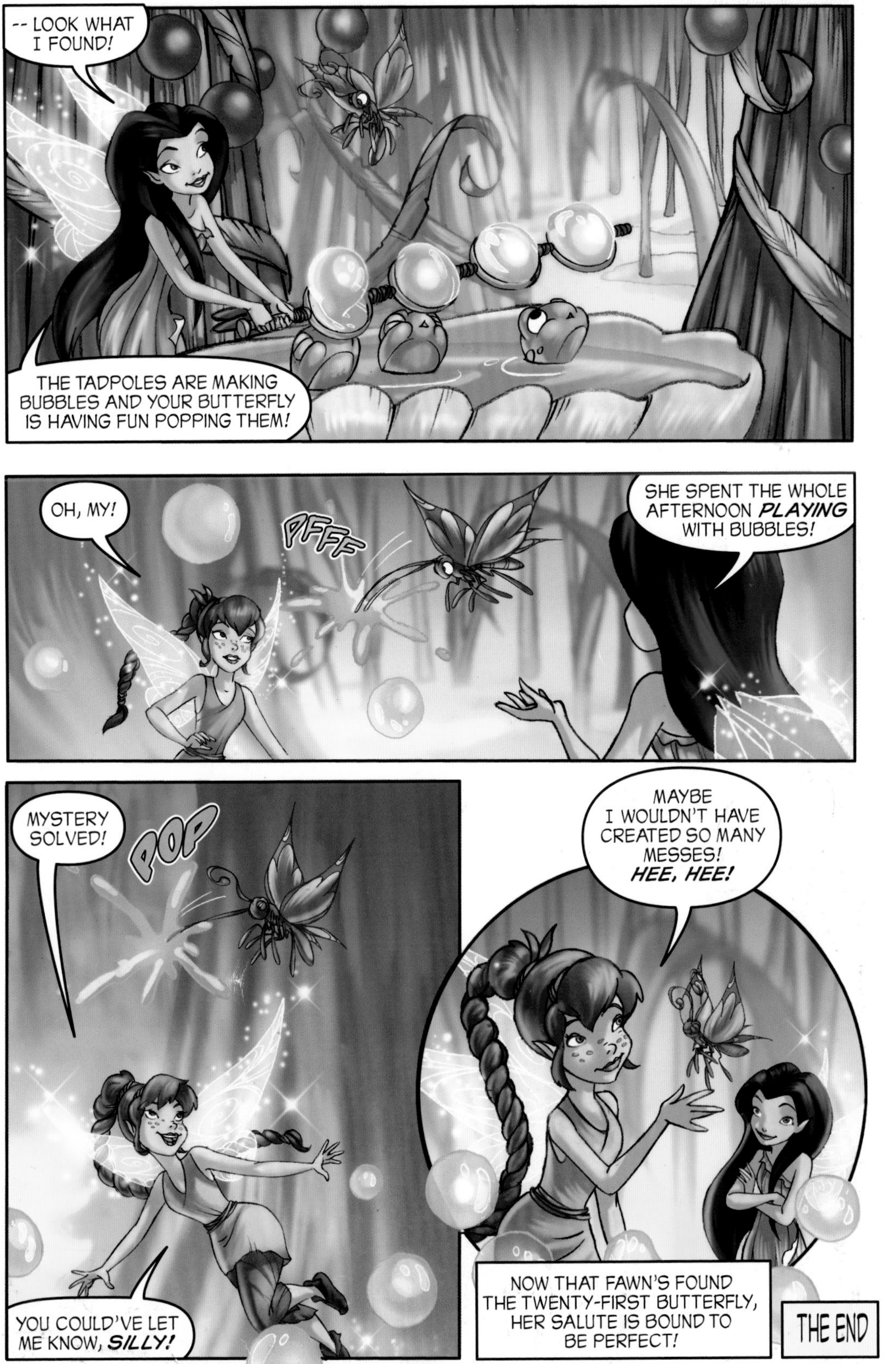
-- LOOK WHAT I FOUND!
THE TADPOLES ARE MAKING BUBBLES AND YOUR BUTTERFLY IS HAVING FUN POPPING THEM!
OH, MY!
PFFF
SHE SPENT THE WHOLE AFTERNOON PLAYING WITH BUBBLES!
MYSTERY SOLVED!
POP
YOU COULD'VE LET ME KNOW, SILLY!
MAYBE I WOULDN'T HAVE CREATED SO MANY MESSES! HEE, HEE!
NOW THAT FAWN'S FOUND THE TWENTY-FIRST BUTTERFLY, HER SALUTE IS BOUND TO BE PERFECT!
THE END

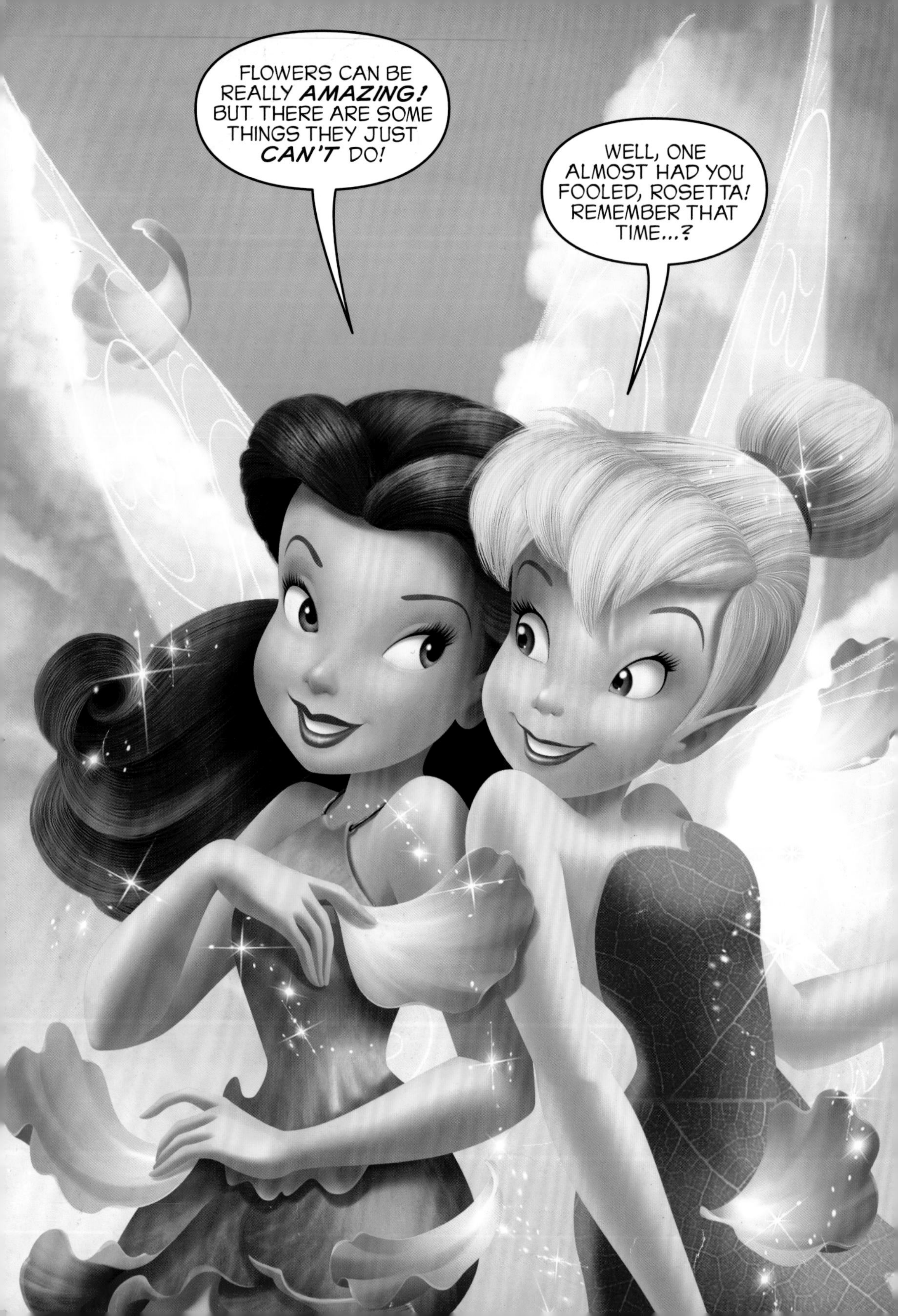
FLOWERS CAN BE REALLY **AMAZING!** BUT THERE ARE SOME THINGS THEY JUST **CAN'T** DO!
WELL, ONE ALMOST HAD YOU FOOLED, ROSETTA! REMEMBER THAT TIME...?

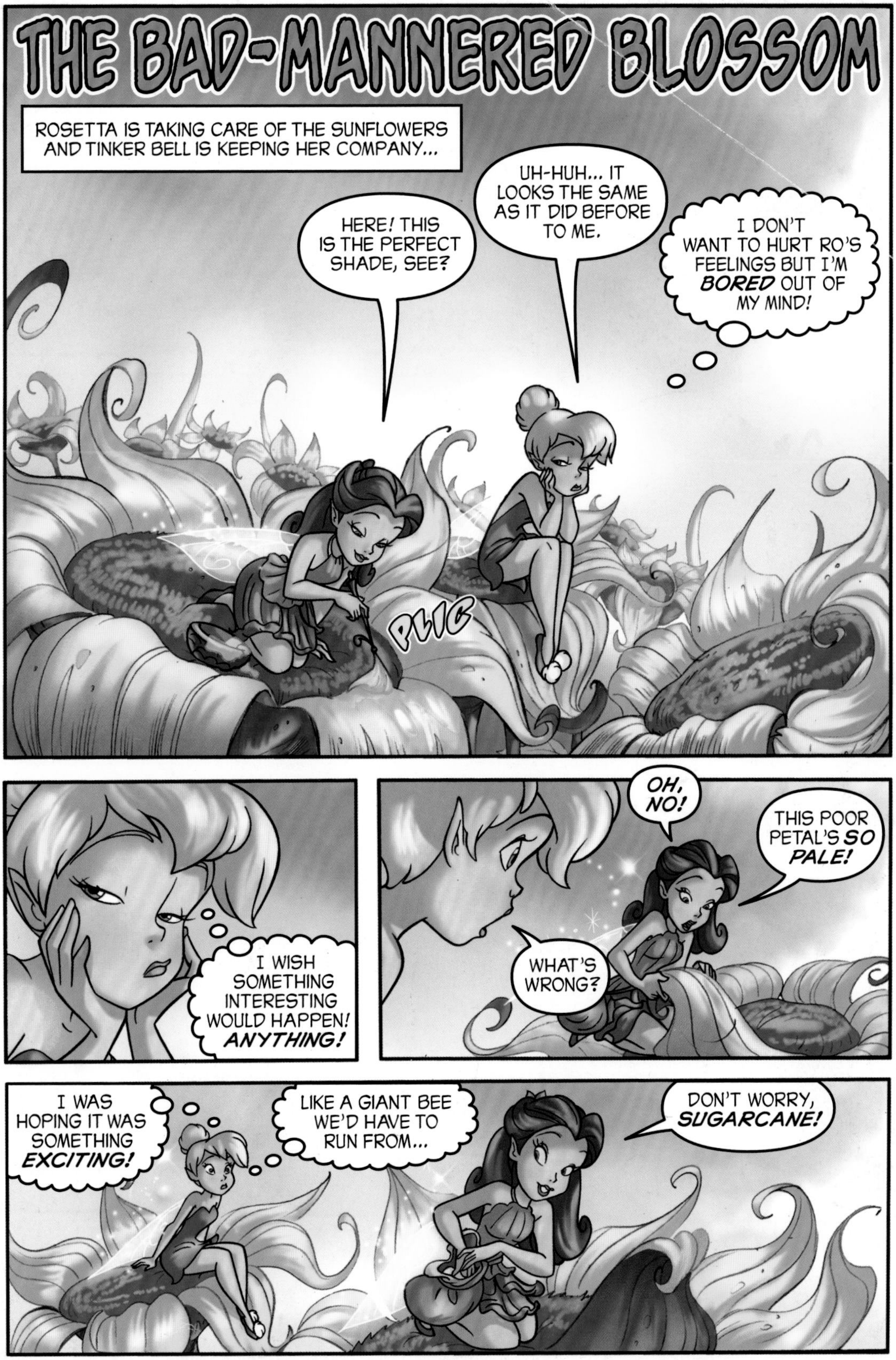
THE BAD-MANNERED BLOSSOM
ROSETTA IS TAKING CARE OF THE SUNFLOWERS AND TINKER BELL IS KEEPING HER COMPANY...
HERE! THIS IS THE PERFECT SHADE, SEE?
UH-HUH... IT LOOKS THE SAME AS IT DID BEFORE TO ME.
I DON'T WANT TO HURT RO'S FEELINGS BUT I'M BORED OUT OF MY MIND!
PLIC
I WISH SOMETHING INTERESTING WOULD HAPPEN! ANYTHING!
OH, NO!
THIS POOR PETAL'S SO PALE!
WHAT'S WRONG?
I WAS HOPING IT WAS SOMETHING EXCITING!
LIKE A GIANT BEE WE'D HAVE TO RUN FROM...
DON'T WORRY, SUGARCANE!

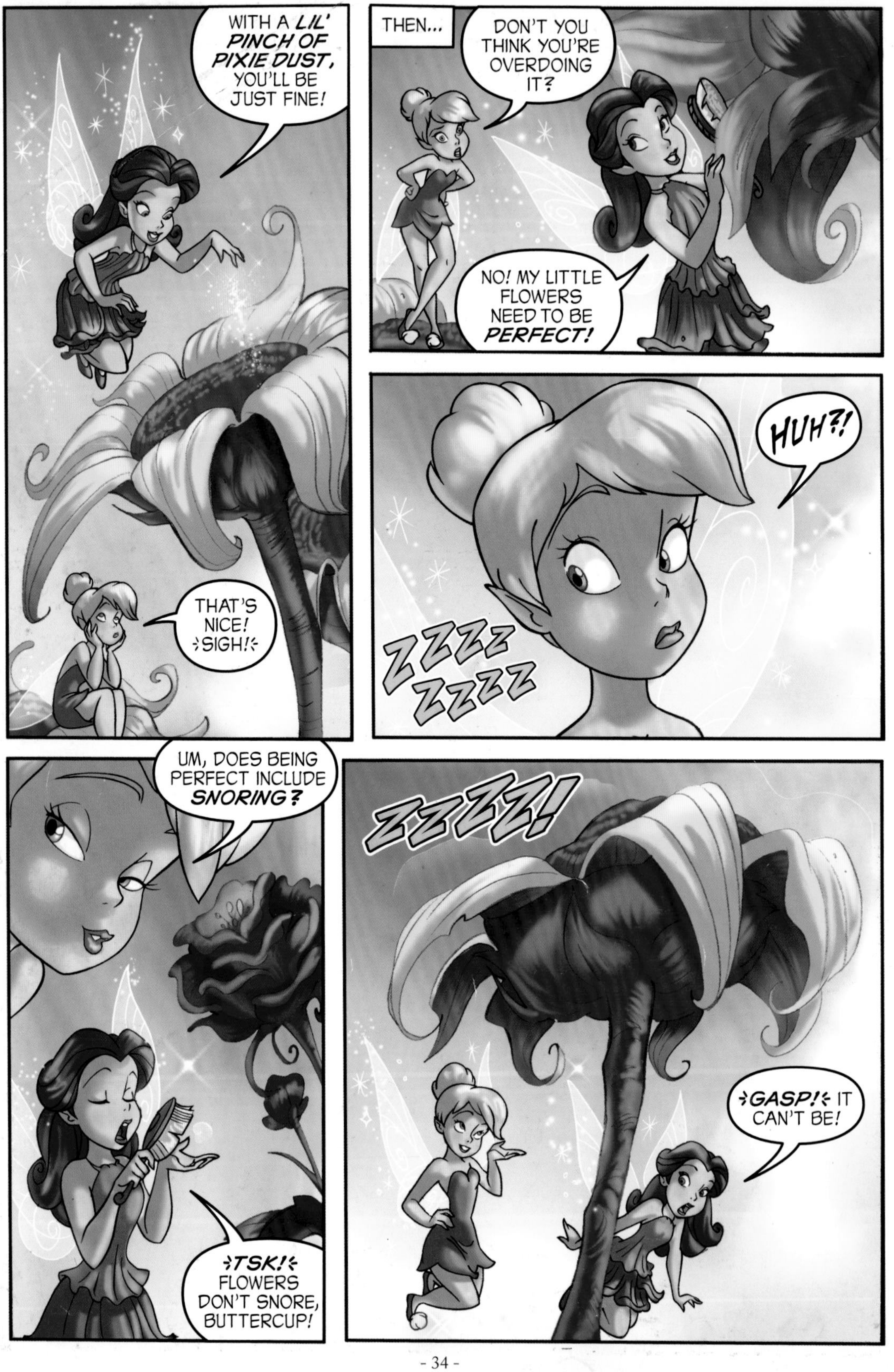
WITH A LIL' PINCH OF PIXIE DUST, YOU'LL BE JUST FINE!
THAT'S NICE! ⁘SIGH!⁘
THEN...
DON'T YOU THINK YOU'RE OVERDOING IT?
NO! MY LITTLE FLOWERS NEED TO BE PERFECT!
HUH?!
ZZZZZ ZZZZ
UM, DOES BEING PERFECT INCLUDE SNORING?
⁘TSK!⁘ FLOWERS DON'T SNORE, BUTTERCUP!
ZZZZZ!
⁘GASP!⁘ IT CAN'T BE!

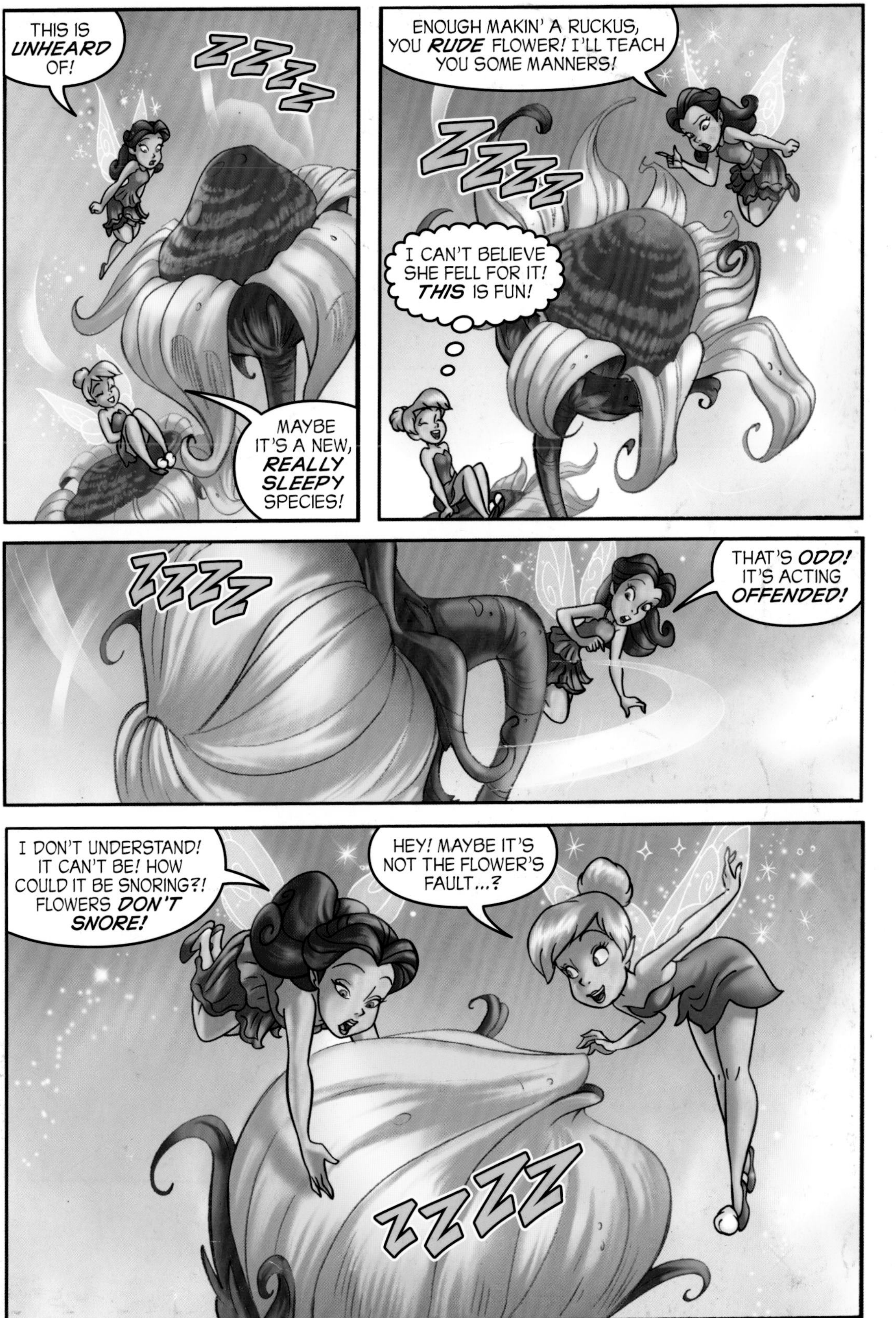
THIS IS UNHEARD OF!
ZZZZ
MAYBE IT'S A NEW, REALLY SLEEPY SPECIES!
ENOUGH MAKIN' A RUCKUS, YOU RUDE FLOWER! I'LL TEACH YOU SOME MANNERS!
ZZZZZ
I CAN'T BELIEVE SHE FELL FOR IT! THIS IS FUN!
ZZZZ
THAT'S ODD! IT'S ACTING OFFENDED!
I DON'T UNDERSTAND! IT CAN'T BE! HOW COULD IT BE SNORING?! FLOWERS DON'T SNORE!
HEY! MAYBE IT'S NOT THE FLOWER'S FAULT...?
ZZZZZ

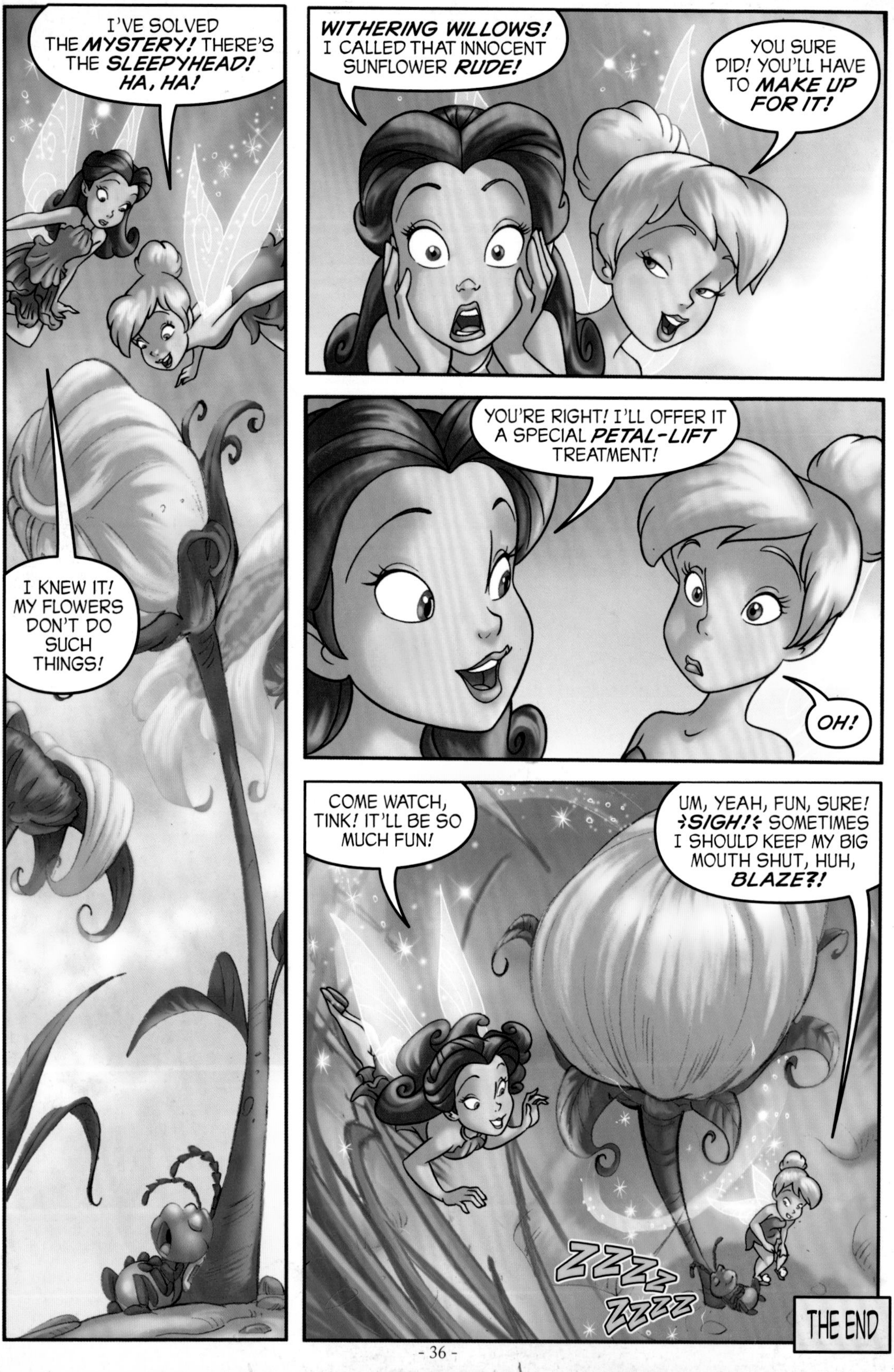
I'VE SOLVED THE MYSTERY! THERE'S THE SLEEPYHEAD! HA, HA!
I KNEW IT! MY FLOWERS DON'T DO SUCH THINGS!
WITHERING WILLOWS! I CALLED THAT INNOCENT SUNFLOWER RUDE!
YOU SURE DID! YOU'LL HAVE TO MAKE UP FOR IT!
YOU'RE RIGHT! I'LL OFFER IT A SPECIAL PETAL-LIFT TREATMENT!
OH!
COME WATCH, TINK! IT'LL BE SO MUCH FUN!
UM, YEAH, FUN, SURE! SIGH! SOMETIMES I SHOULD KEEP MY BIG MOUTH SHUT, HUH, BLAZE?!
ZZZZ ZZZZ
THE END

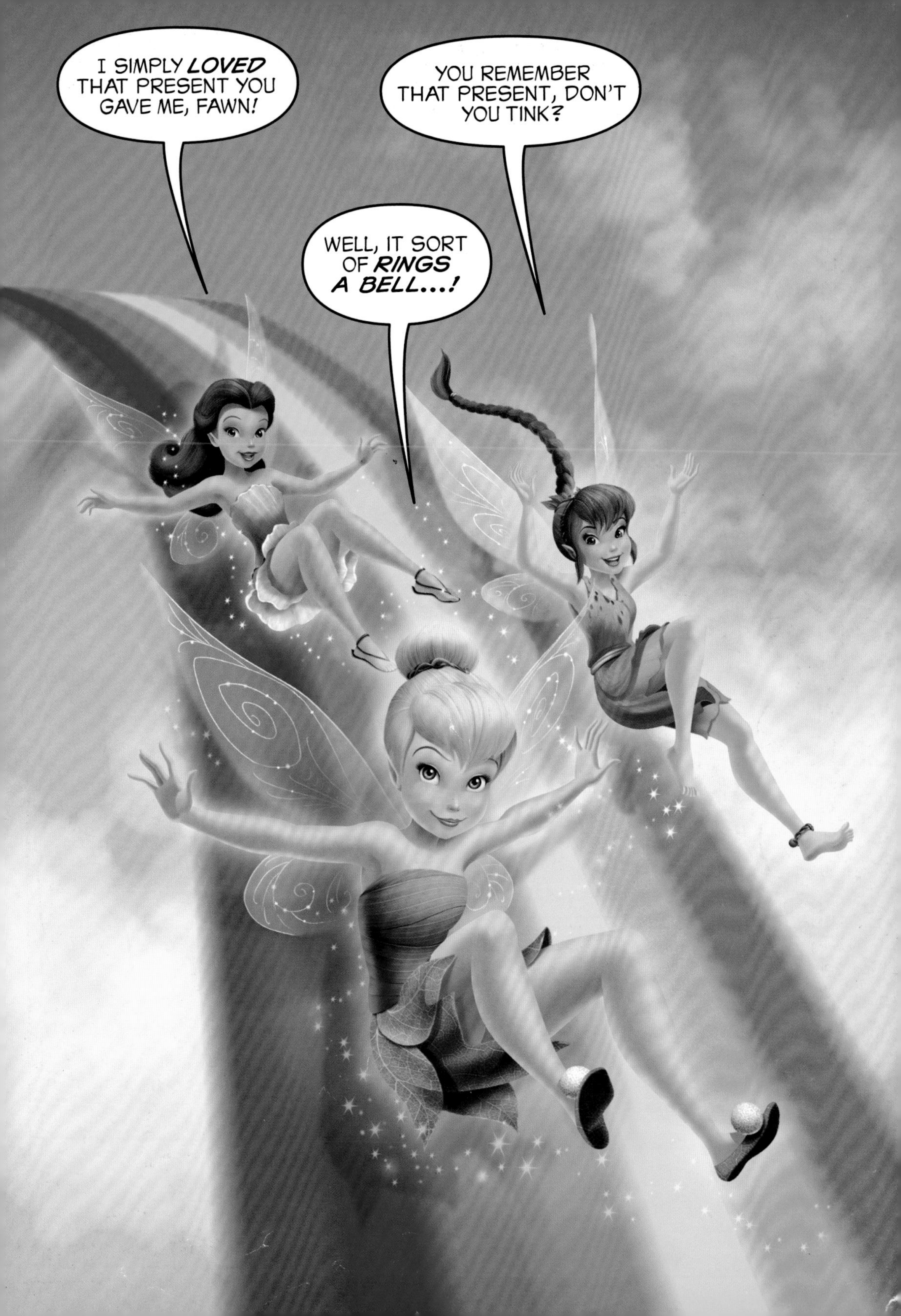
I SIMPLY LOVED THAT PRESENT YOU GAVE ME, FAWN!
YOU REMEMBER THAT PRESENT, DON'T YOU TINK?
WELL, IT SORT OF RINGS A BELL...!

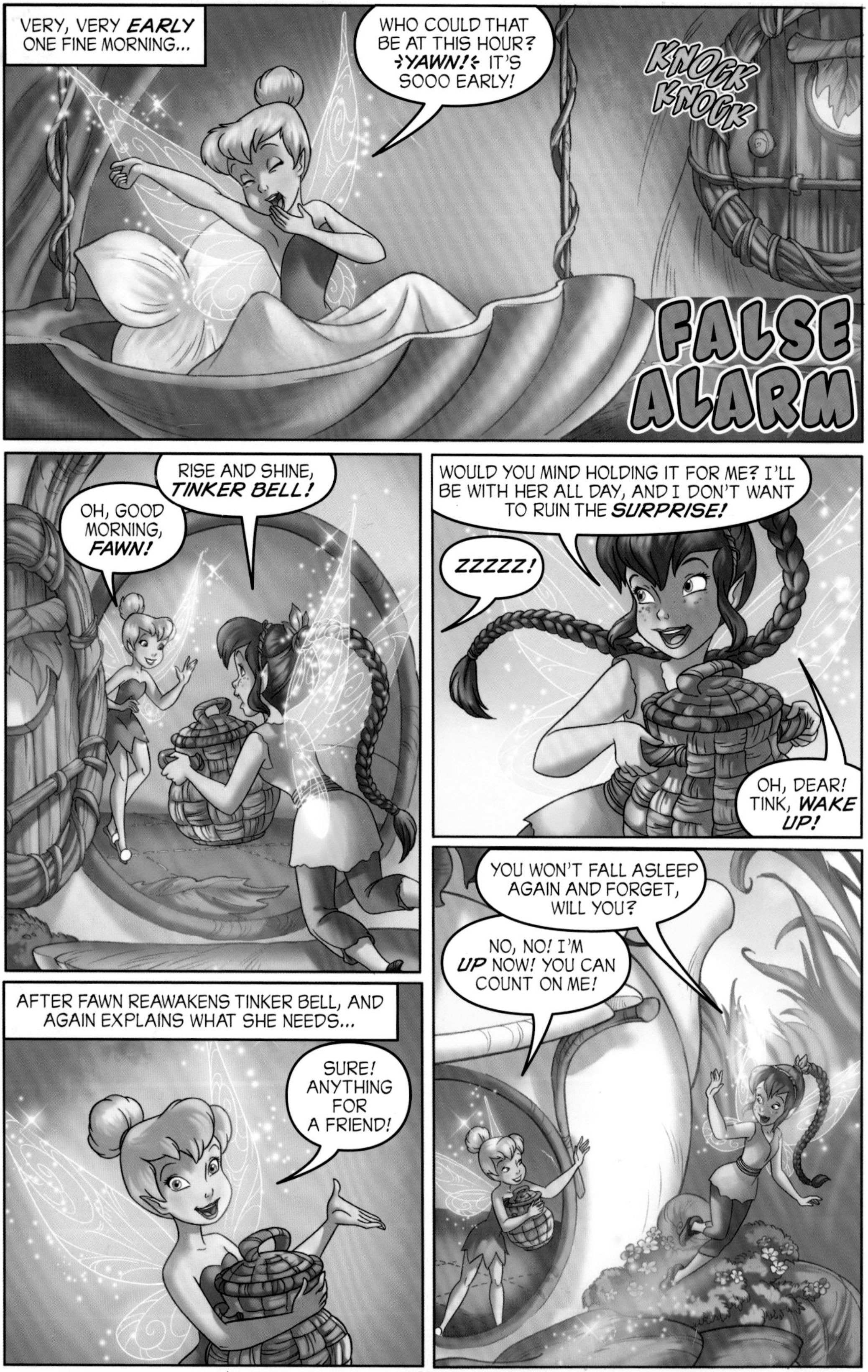

VERY, VERY *EARLY* ONE FINE MORNING...
WHO COULD THAT BE AT THIS HOUR? *YAWN!* IT'S SOOO EARLY!
KNOCK KNOCK
FALSE ALARM
RISE AND SHINE, *TINKER BELL!*
OH, GOOD MORNING, *FAWN!*
WOULD YOU MIND HOLDING IT FOR ME? I'LL BE WITH HER ALL DAY, AND I DON'T WANT TO RUIN THE *SURPRISE!*
ZZZZZ!
OH, DEAR! TINK, *WAKE UP!*
AFTER FAWN REAWAKENS TINKER BELL, AND AGAIN EXPLAINS WHAT SHE NEEDS...
SURE! ANYTHING FOR A FRIEND!
YOU WON'T FALL ASLEEP AGAIN AND FORGET, WILL YOU?
NO, NO! I'M *UP* NOW! YOU CAN COUNT ON ME!

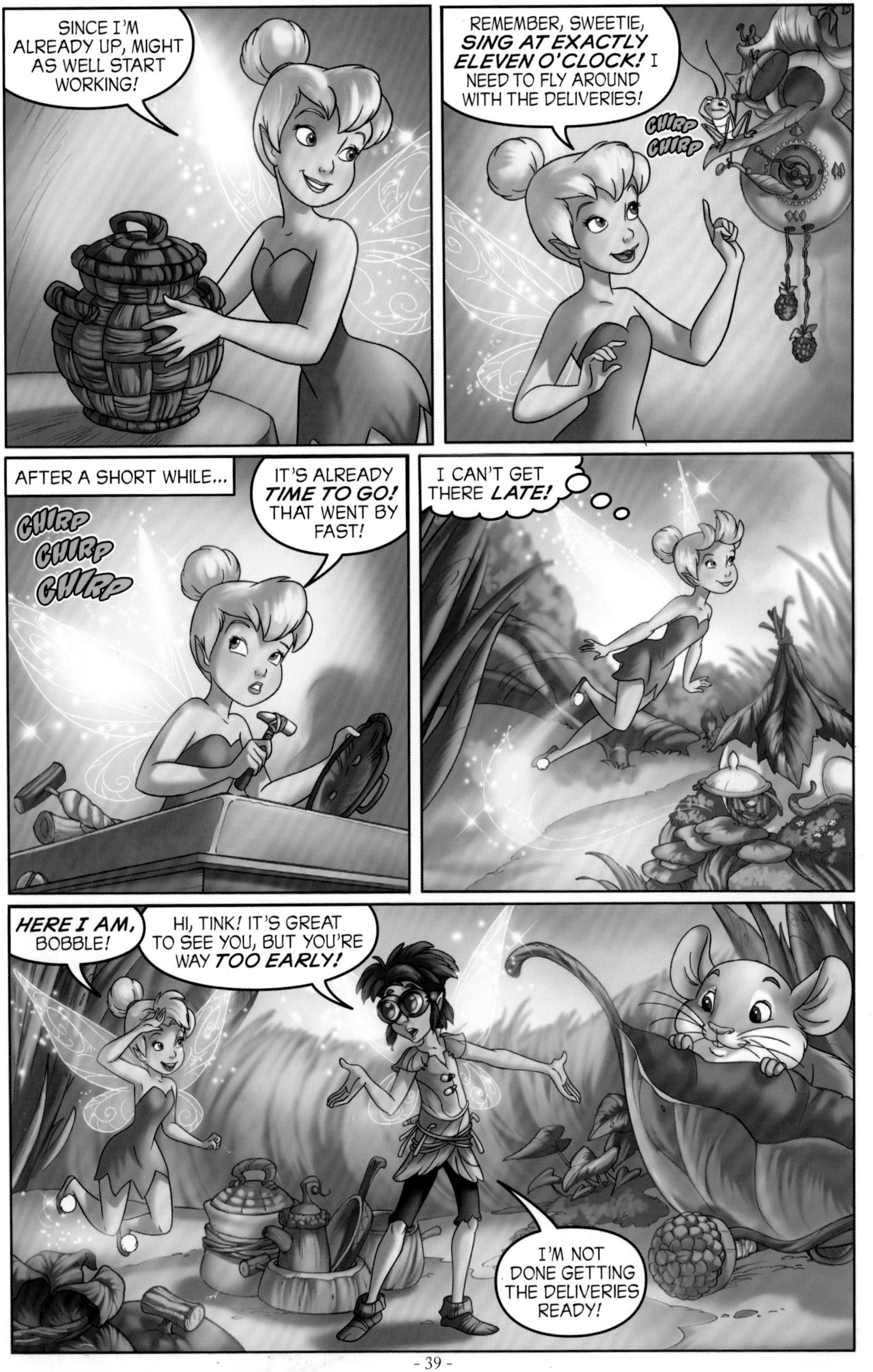

SINCE I'M ALREADY UP, MIGHT AS WELL START WORKING!
REMEMBER, SWEETIE, **SING AT EXACTLY ELEVEN O'CLOCK!** I NEED TO FLY AROUND WITH THE DELIVERIES!
CHIRP CHIRP
AFTER A SHORT WHILE...
CHIRP CHIRP CHIRP
IT'S ALREADY **TIME TO GO!** THAT WENT BY FAST!
I CAN'T GET THERE **LATE!**
HERE I AM, BOBBLE!
HI, TINK! IT'S GREAT TO SEE YOU, BUT YOU'RE WAY **TOO EARLY!**
I'M NOT DONE GETTING THE DELIVERIES READY!

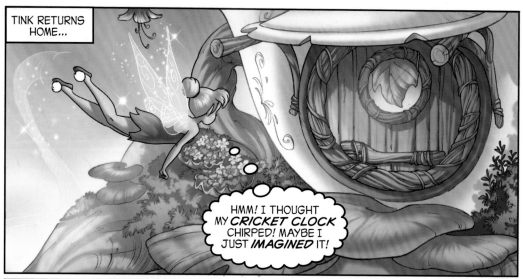

TINK RETURNS HOME...

HMM! I THOUGHT MY *CRICKET CLOCK* CHIRPED! MAYBE I JUST *IMAGINED* IT!

I'LL GET BACK TO WO--

CHIRP CHIRP

THAT WAS MY *CRICKET!* TIME TO GO!

IN A WINGBEAT, TINK IS BACK IN TINKERS' NOOK!

I'M *READY* TO MAKE THE DELIVERIES!

TINK?! YOU'LL NEED TO WAIT! YOU'RE *STILL TOO EARLY!*

SOMETHING'S NOT *CRICKET!*

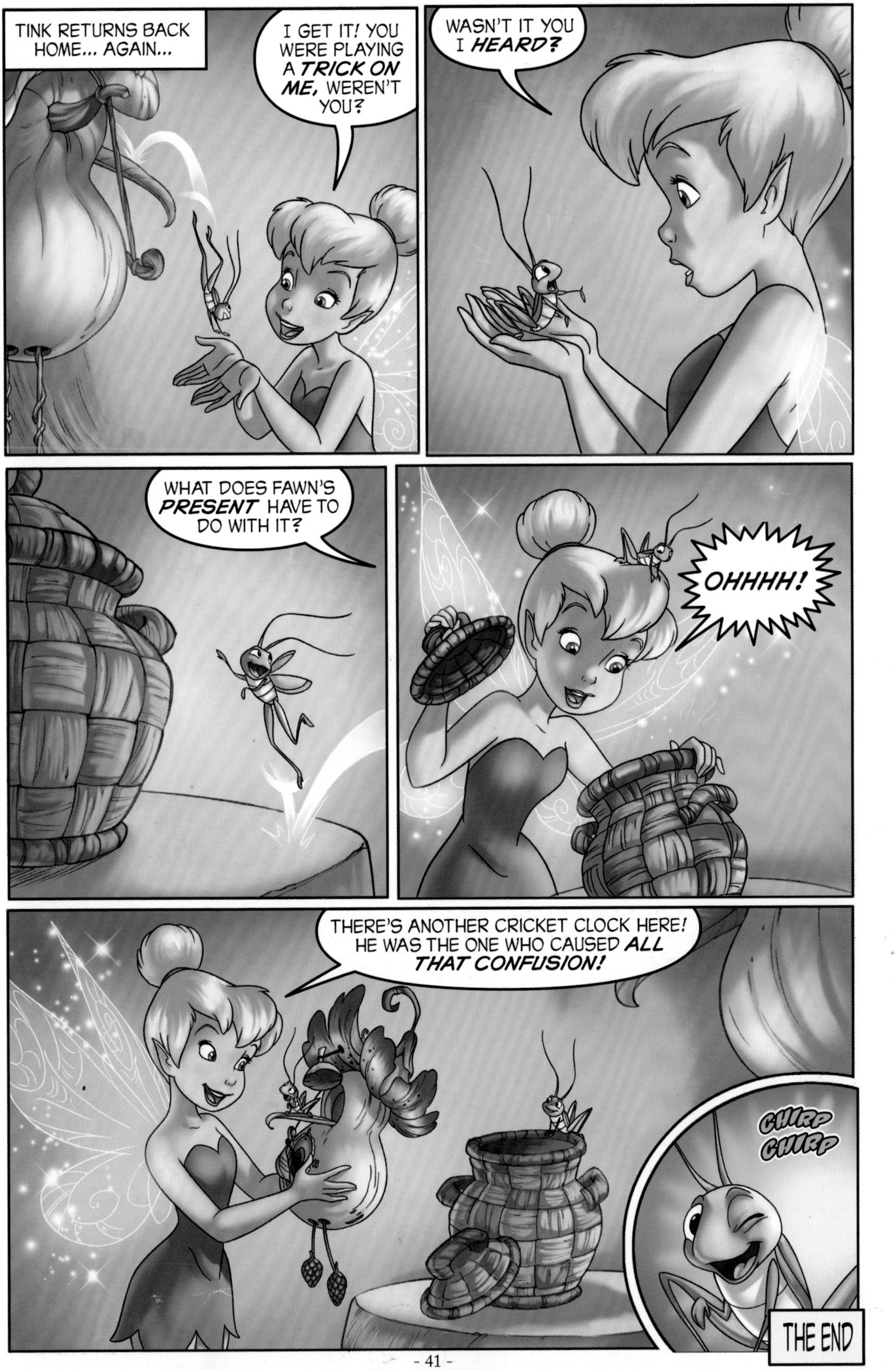
TINK RETURNS BACK HOME... AGAIN...
I GET IT! YOU WERE PLAYING A TRICK ON ME, WEREN'T YOU?
WASN'T IT YOU I HEARD?
WHAT DOES FAWN'S PRESENT HAVE TO DO WITH IT?
OHHHH!
THERE'S ANOTHER CRICKET CLOCK HERE! HE WAS THE ONE WHO CAUSED ALL THAT CONFUSION!
CHIRP CHIRP
THE END

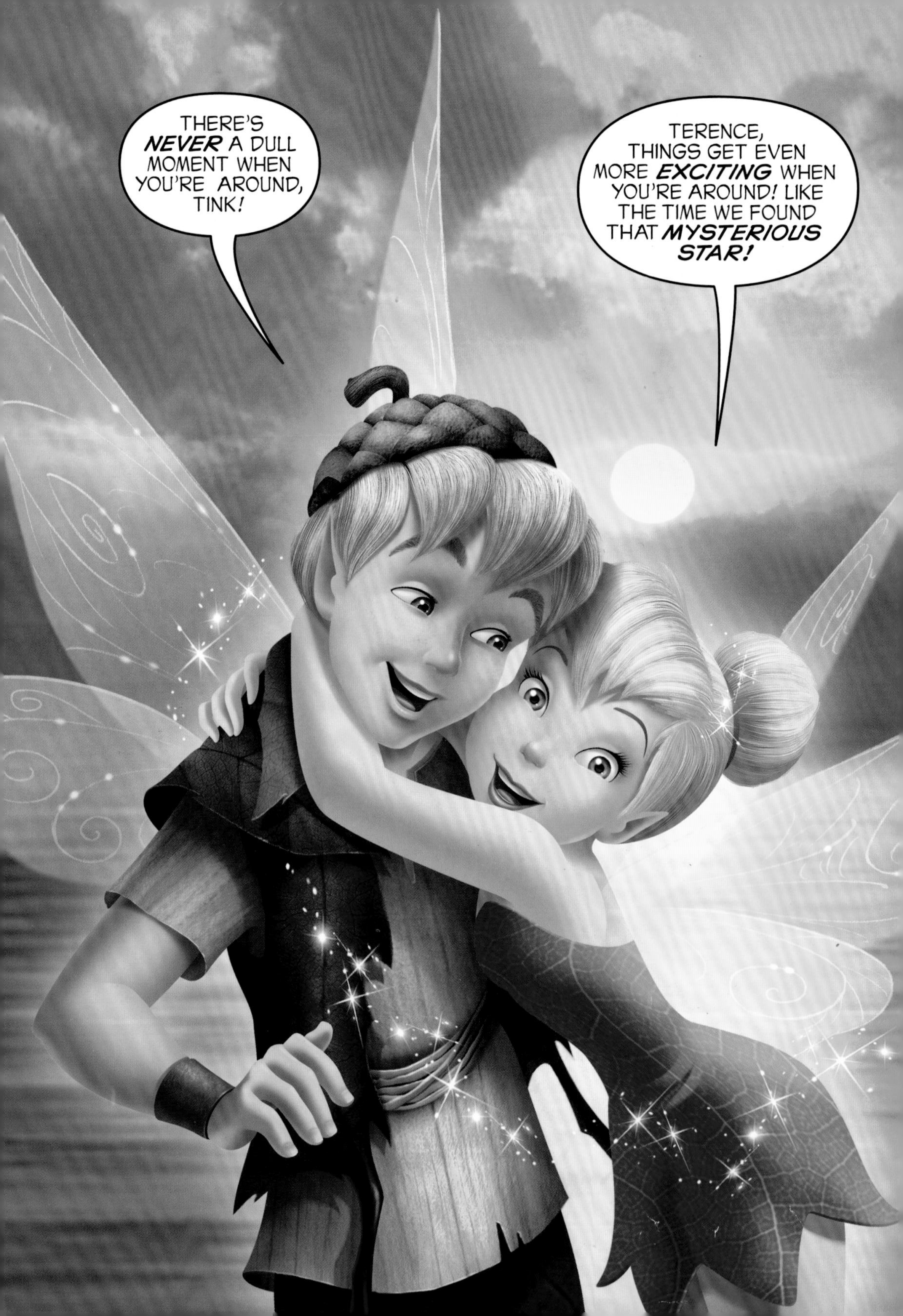
THERE'S *NEVER* A DULL MOMENT WHEN YOU'RE AROUND, TINK!
TERENCE, THINGS GET EVEN MORE *EXCITING* WHEN YOU'RE AROUND! LIKE THE TIME WE FOUND THAT *MYSTERIOUS STAR!*

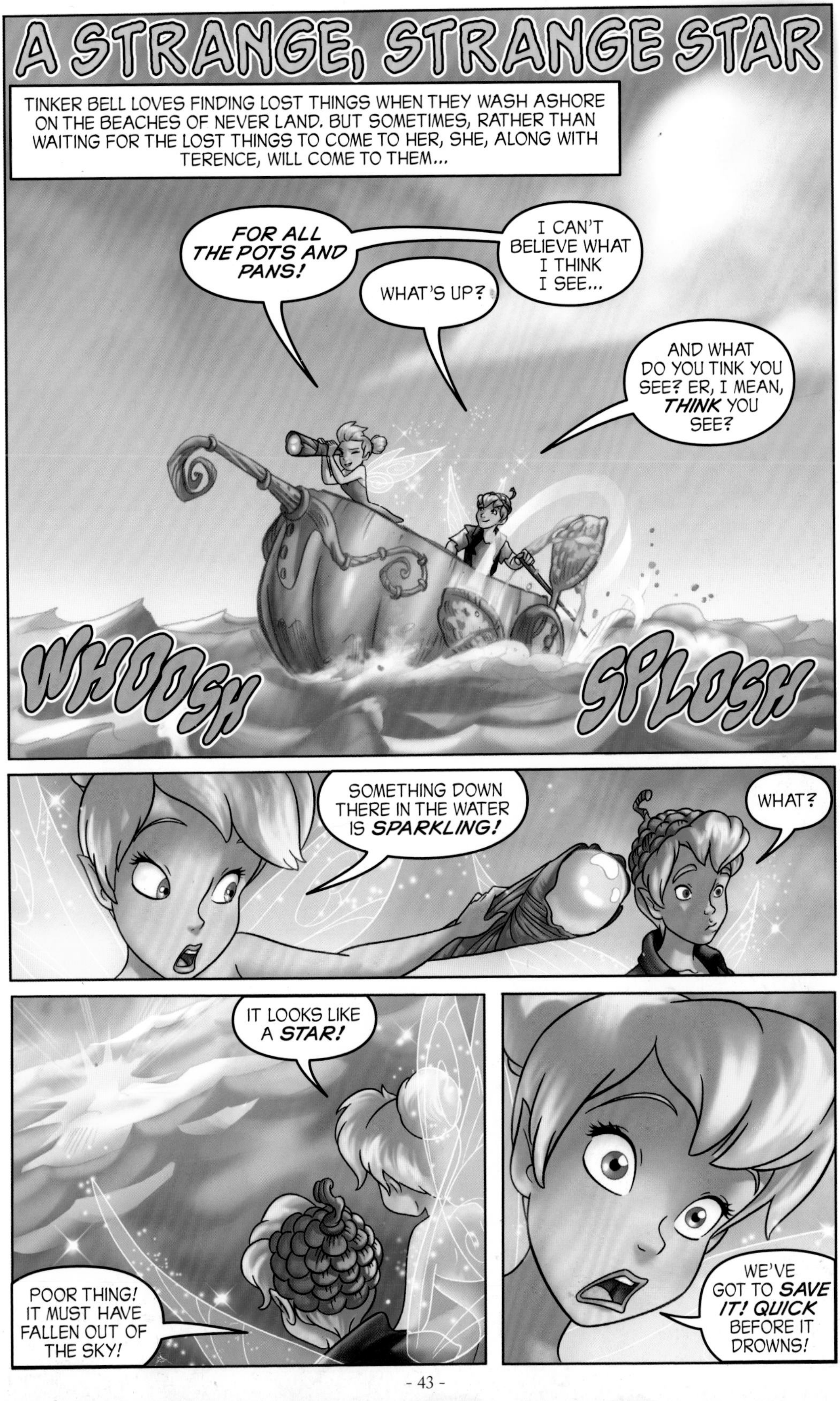
A STRANGE, STRANGE STAR
TINKER BELL LOVES FINDING LOST THINGS WHEN THEY WASH ASHORE ON THE BEACHES OF NEVER LAND. BUT SOMETIMES, RATHER THAN WAITING FOR THE LOST THINGS TO COME TO HER, SHE, ALONG WITH TERENCE, WILL COME TO THEM...
FOR ALL THE POTS AND PANS!
I CAN'T BELIEVE WHAT I THINK I SEE...
WHAT'S UP?
AND WHAT DO YOU TINK YOU SEE? ER, I MEAN, THINK YOU SEE?
WHOOSH
SPLOSH
SOMETHING DOWN THERE IN THE WATER IS SPARKLING!
WHAT?
IT LOOKS LIKE A STAR!
POOR THING! IT MUST HAVE FALLEN OUT OF THE SKY!
WE'VE GOT TO SAVE IT! QUICK BEFORE IT DROWNS!

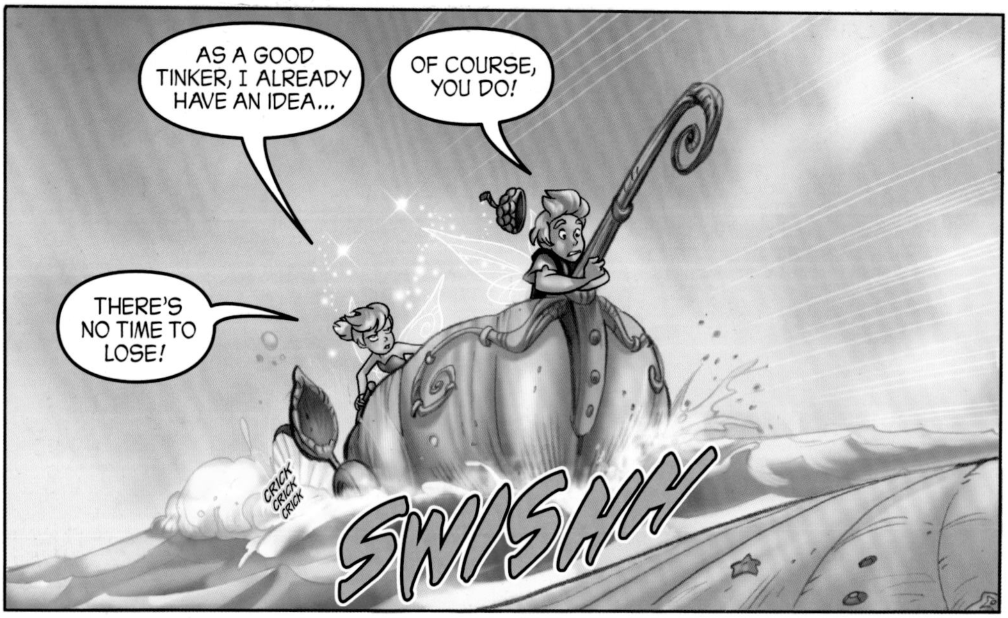
AS A GOOD TINKER, I ALREADY HAVE AN IDEA...
OF COURSE, YOU DO!
THERE'S NO TIME TO LOSE!
CRICK CRICK CRICK
SWISHH

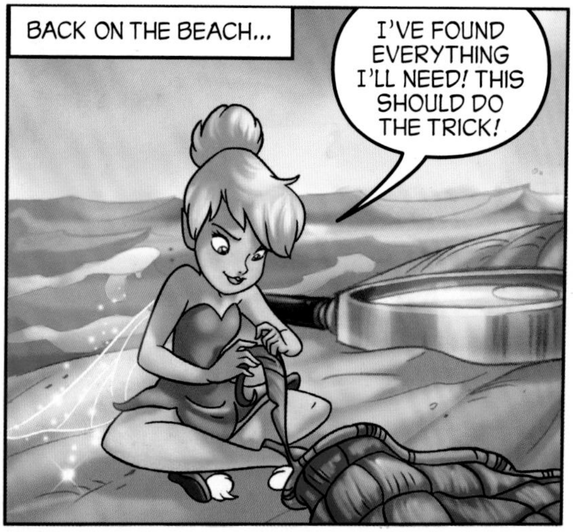
BACK ON THE BEACH...
I'VE FOUND EVERYTHING I'LL NEED! THIS SHOULD DO THE TRICK!

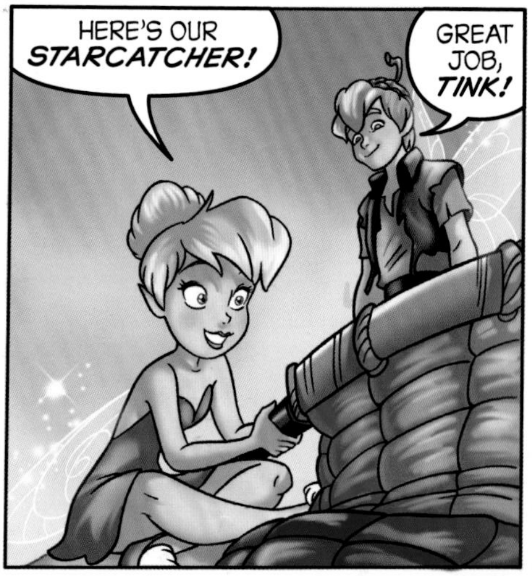
HERE'S OUR STARCATCHER!
GREAT JOB, TINK!

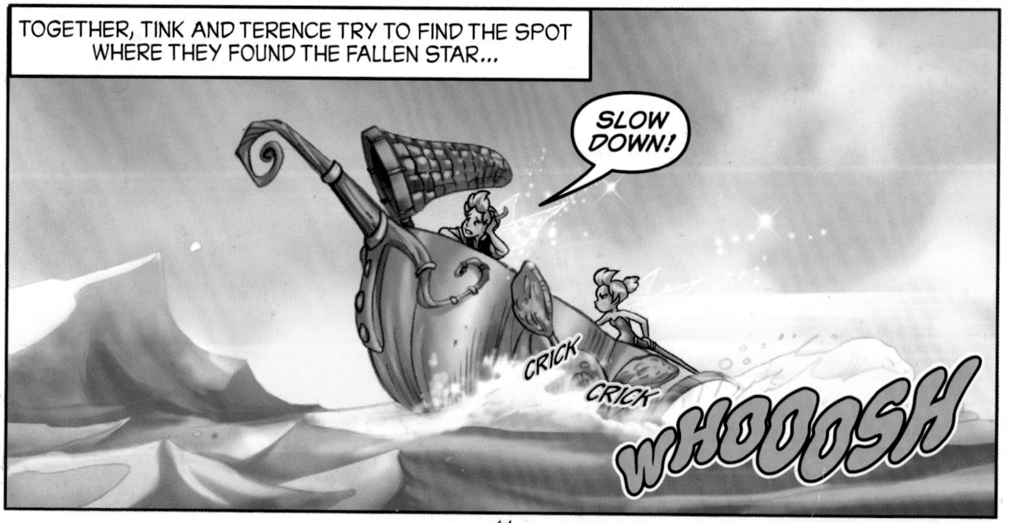
TOGETHER, TINK AND TERENCE TRY TO FIND THE SPOT WHERE THEY FOUND THE FALLEN STAR...
SLOW DOWN!
CRICK
CRICK
WHOOOSH

A WINGBEAT LATER...

I GOT IT! ⸙PANT!⸙

AND...

⸙MFF!⸙ YOU'D THINK A STAR WOULD BE LIGHT, RIGHT?

IT'S A LOT HEAVIER THAN I EXPECTED!

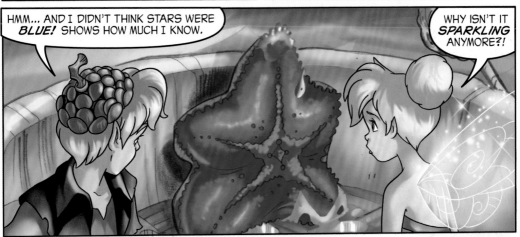

HMM... AND I DIDN'T THINK STARS WERE *BLUE!* SHOWS HOW MUCH I KNOW.

WHY ISN'T IT *SPARKLING* ANYMORE?!

IT PROBABLY NEEDS TO GET BACK IN THE SKY! LET'S TAKE IT TO *IRIDESSA!*

SHE KNOWS ALL ABOUT LIGHT AND STARS!

AND SO...

WATCH YOUR STEP!

HEY, WHERE ARE YOU TAKING THAT POOR *STARFISH?*

SILVERMIST— DID YOU SAY "STARFISH"?!
IT WAS SPARKLING LIKE A STAR IN THE SKY, AND WE THOUGHT IT MUST HAVE FALLEN.
HEEE HEEE! NO, SILLY...
SOME LITTLE STARFISH LIGHT UP WHEN THEY MOVE ACROSS THE DARK SEA FLOOR!
GULP! WE'VE GOT TO GET IT BACK INTO THE WATER!
AND SO, BACK AT SEA...
THERE!
SPLOSH
LOOK AT IT GLOW!
IT'S SAYING GOODBYE!
BYE, CUTIE! I PROMISE WE WON'T FISH FOR YOU ANYMORE! HA, HA!
NATURE IS ALWAYS FULL OF WONDERFUL SURPRISES. TODAY, TINKER BELL AND TERENCE DISCOVERED ONE OF THEM...
THE END

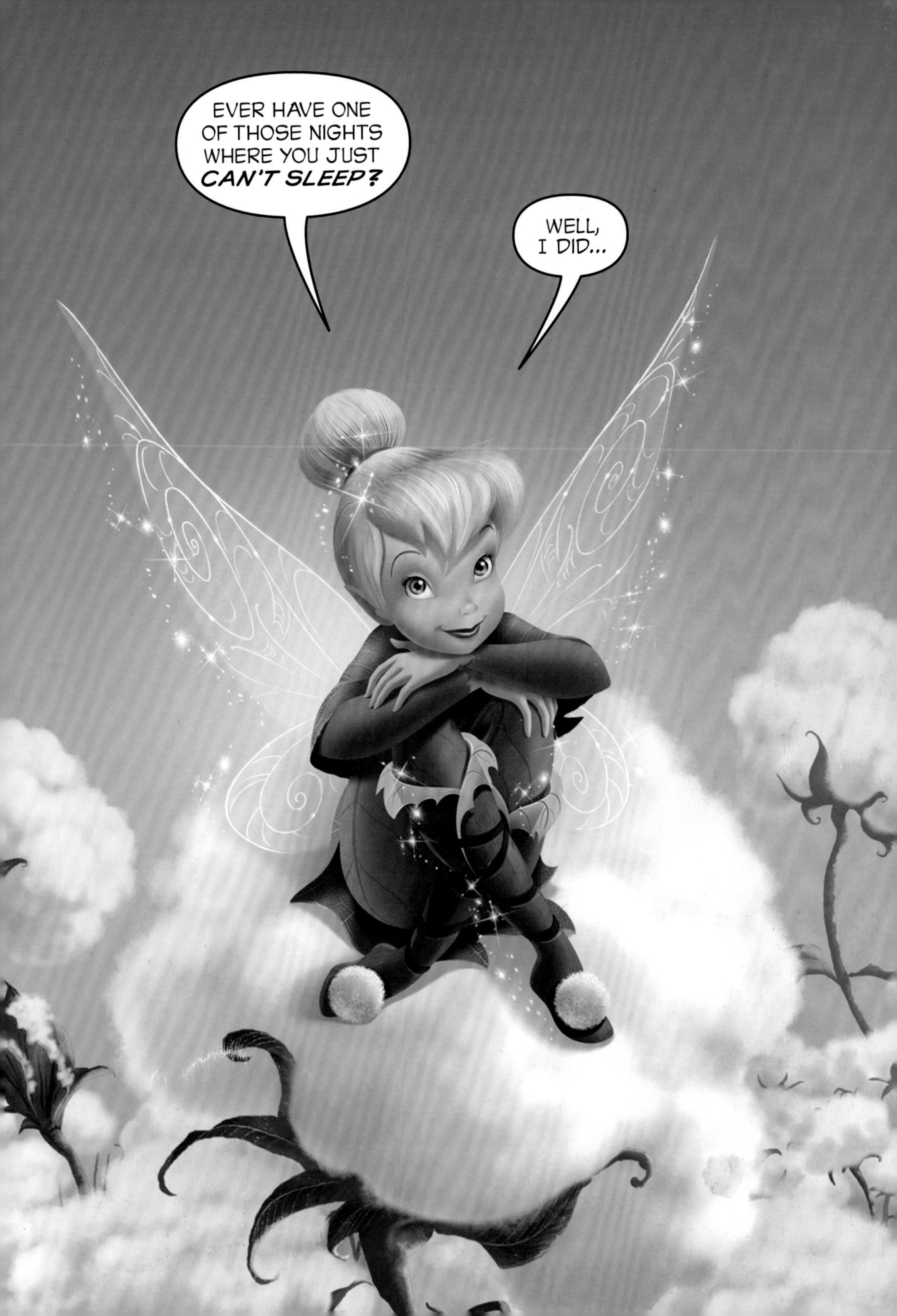
EVER HAVE ONE OF THOSE NIGHTS WHERE YOU JUST *CAN'T SLEEP?*
WELL, I DID...

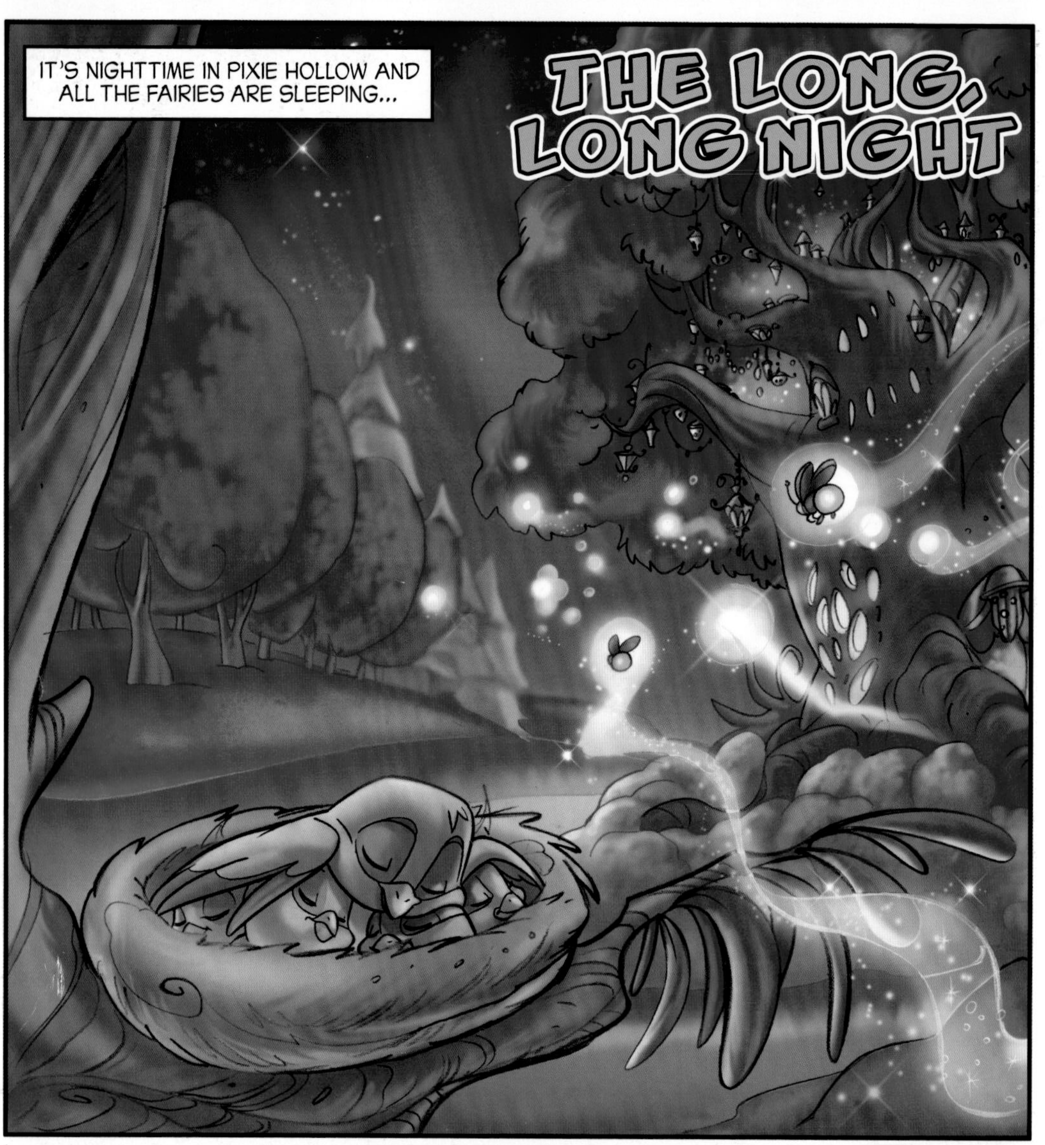
IT'S NIGHTTIME IN PIXIE HOLLOW AND ALL THE FAIRIES ARE SLEEPING...
THE LONG, LONG NIGHT

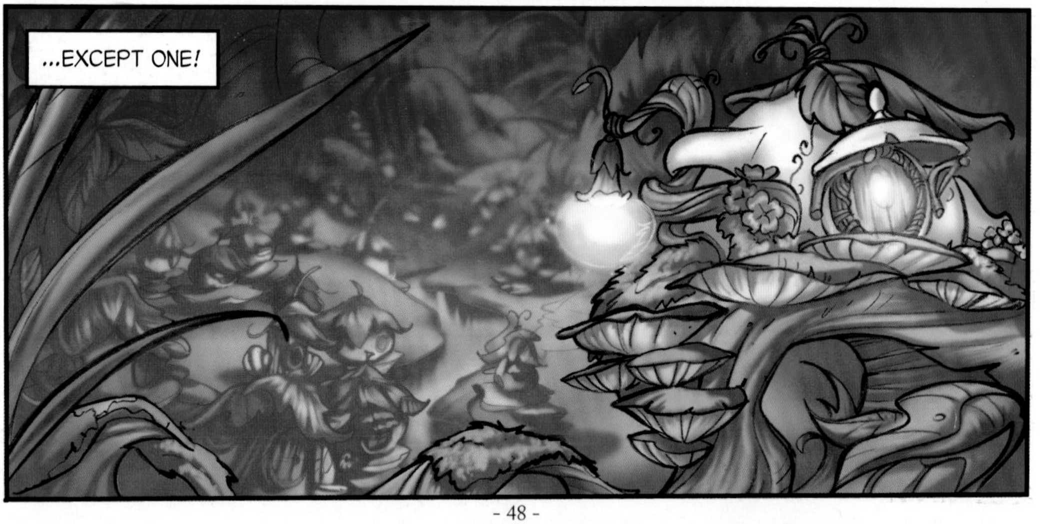
...EXCEPT ONE!

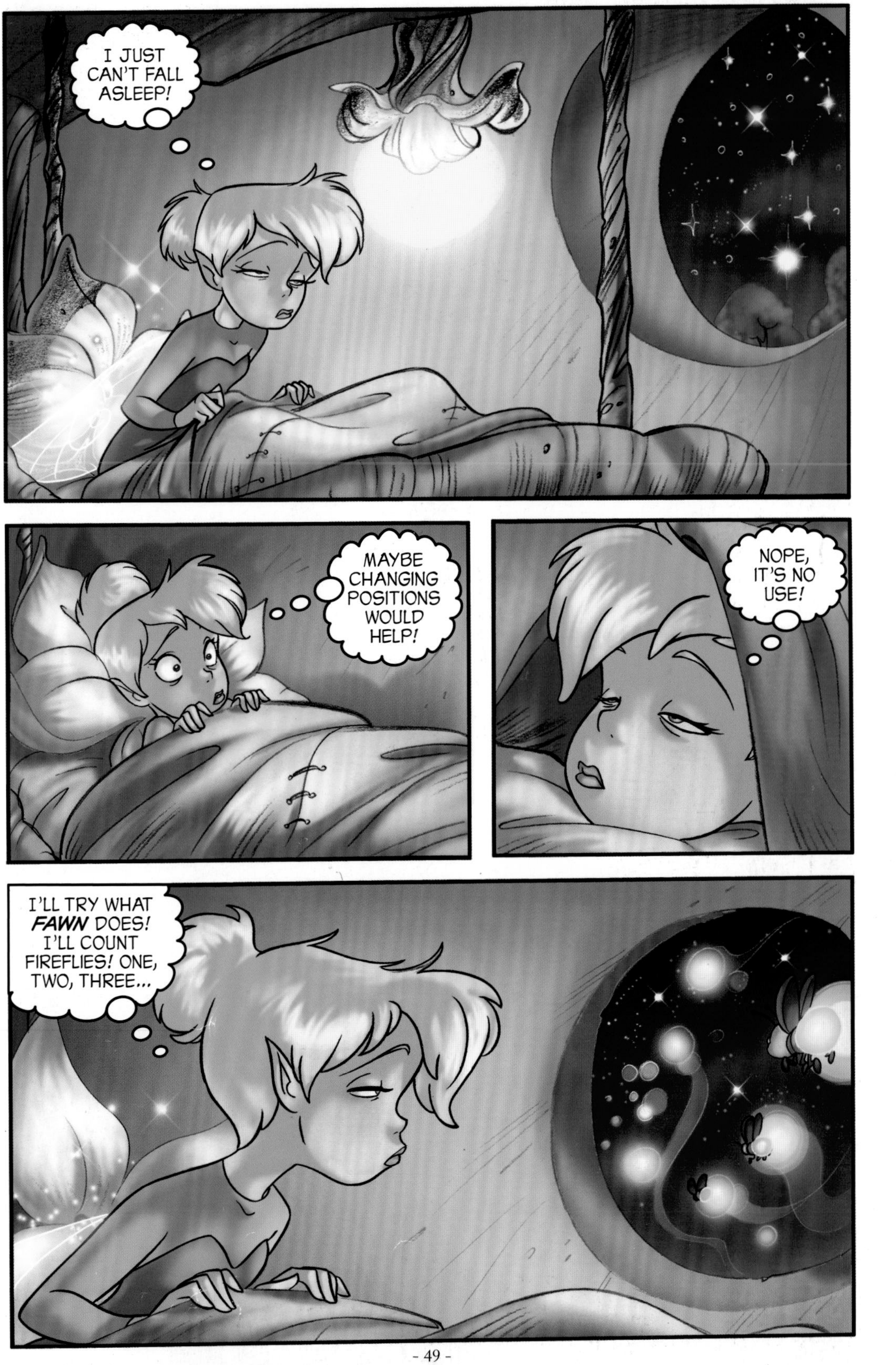
I JUST CAN'T FALL ASLEEP!
MAYBE CHANGING POSITIONS WOULD HELP!
NOPE, IT'S NO USE!
I'LL TRY WHAT ***FAWN*** DOES! I'LL COUNT FIREFLIES! ONE, TWO, THREE...

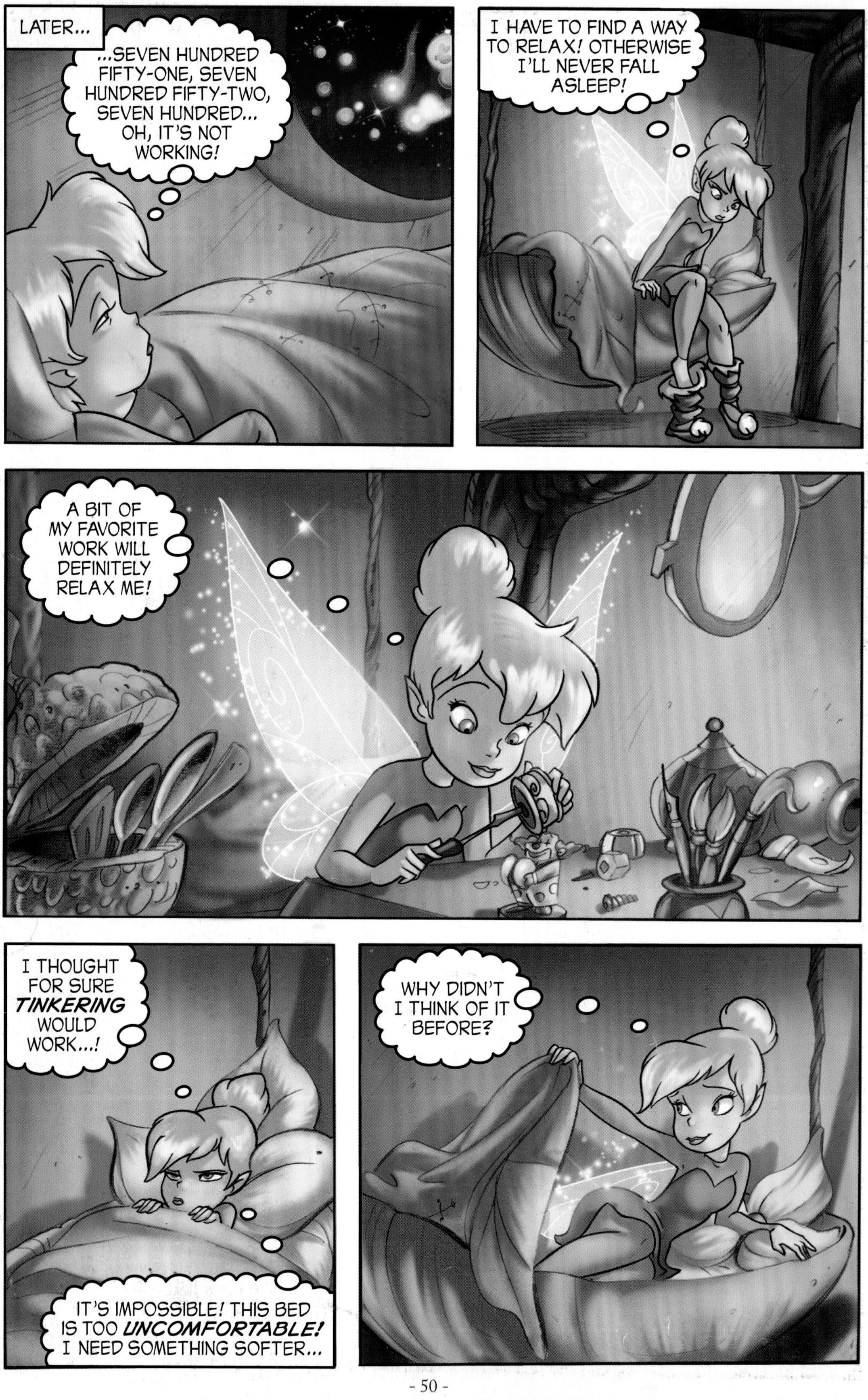
LATER...
...SEVEN HUNDRED FIFTY-ONE, SEVEN HUNDRED FIFTY-TWO, SEVEN HUNDRED... OH, IT'S NOT WORKING!
I HAVE TO FIND A WAY TO RELAX! OTHERWISE I'LL NEVER FALL ASLEEP!
A BIT OF MY FAVORITE WORK WILL DEFINITELY RELAX ME!
I THOUGHT FOR SURE *TINKERING* WOULD WORK...!
IT'S IMPOSSIBLE! THIS BED IS TOO *UNCOMFORTABLE!* I NEED SOMETHING SOFTER...
WHY DIDN'T I THINK OF IT BEFORE?

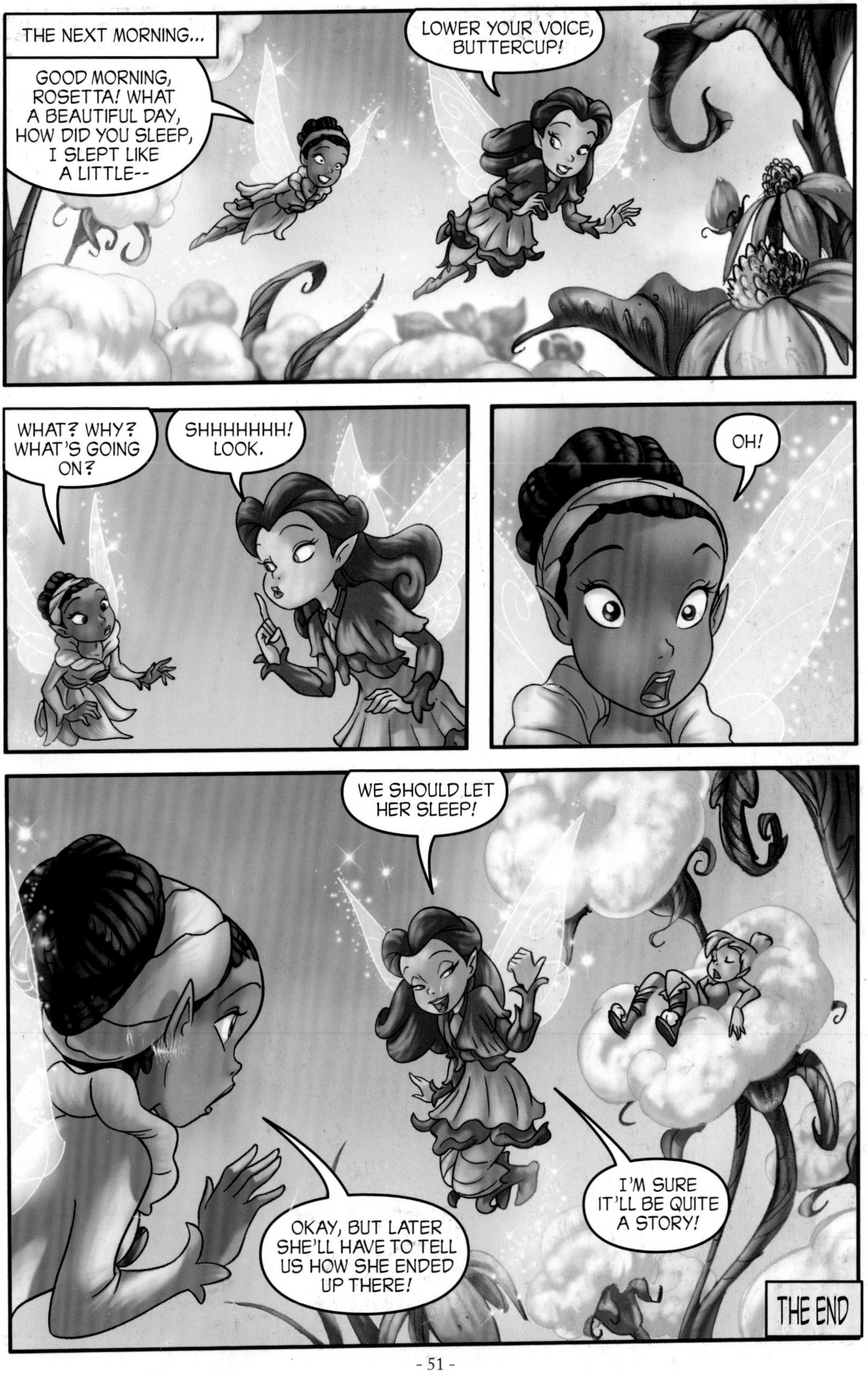

THE NEXT MORNING...
GOOD MORNING, ROSETTA! WHAT A BEAUTIFUL DAY, HOW DID YOU SLEEP, I SLEPT LIKE A LITTLE--
LOWER YOUR VOICE, BUTTERCUP!
WHAT? WHY? WHAT'S GOING ON?
SHHHHHHH! LOOK.
OH!
WE SHOULD LET HER SLEEP!
OKAY, BUT LATER SHE'LL HAVE TO TELL US HOW SHE ENDED UP THERE!
I'M SURE IT'LL BE QUITE A STORY!
THE END

WOW! LOOK AT ALL THE STARS TONIGHT!
NOW YOU KNOW WHY THAT'S A VERY GOOD THING!

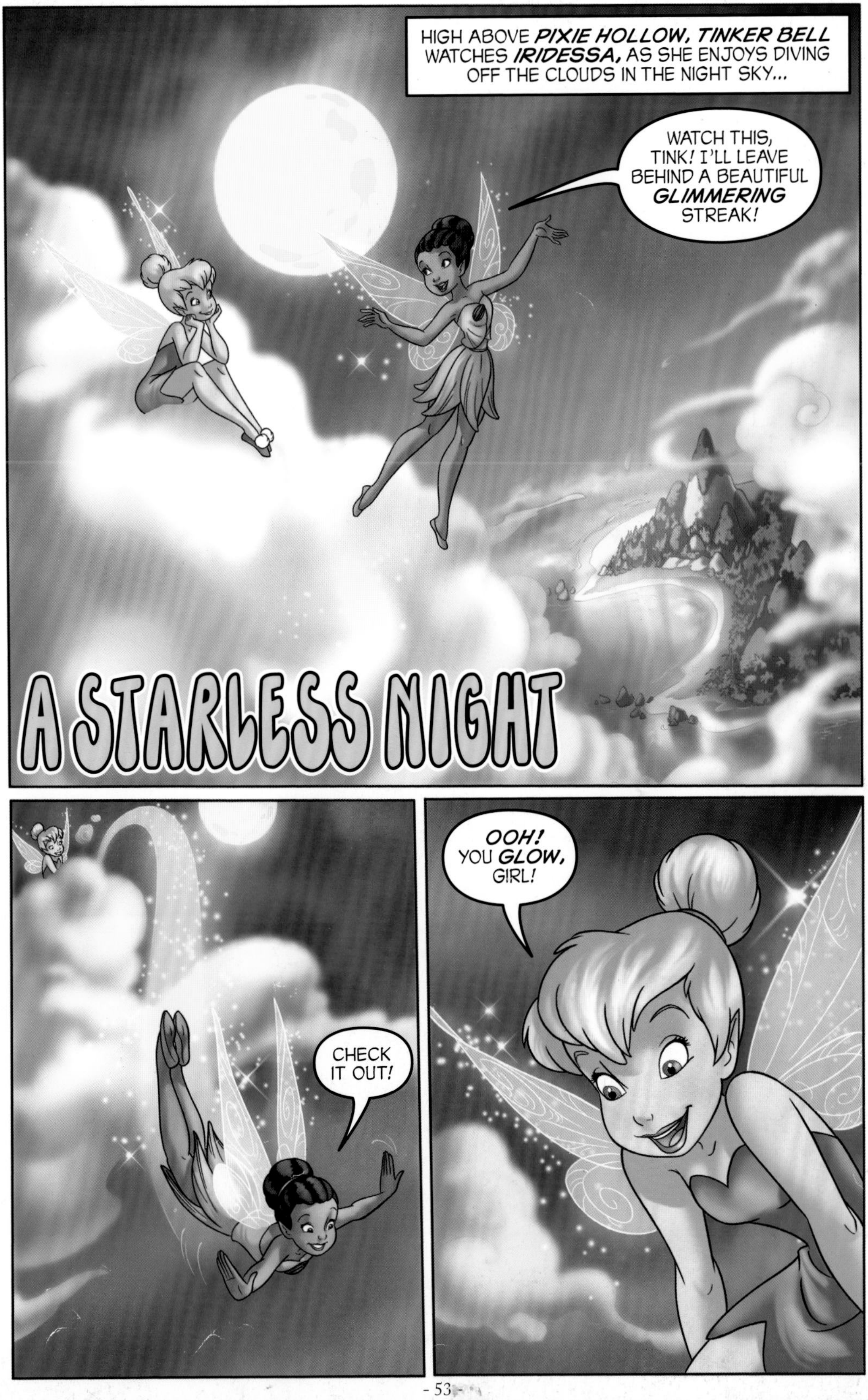
HIGH ABOVE PIXIE HOLLOW, TINKER BELL WATCHES IRIDESSA, AS SHE ENJOYS DIVING OFF THE CLOUDS IN THE NIGHT SKY...
WATCH THIS, TINK! I'LL LEAVE BEHIND A BEAUTIFUL GLIMMERING STREAK!
A STARLESS NIGHT
CHECK IT OUT!
OOH! YOU GLOW, GIRL!

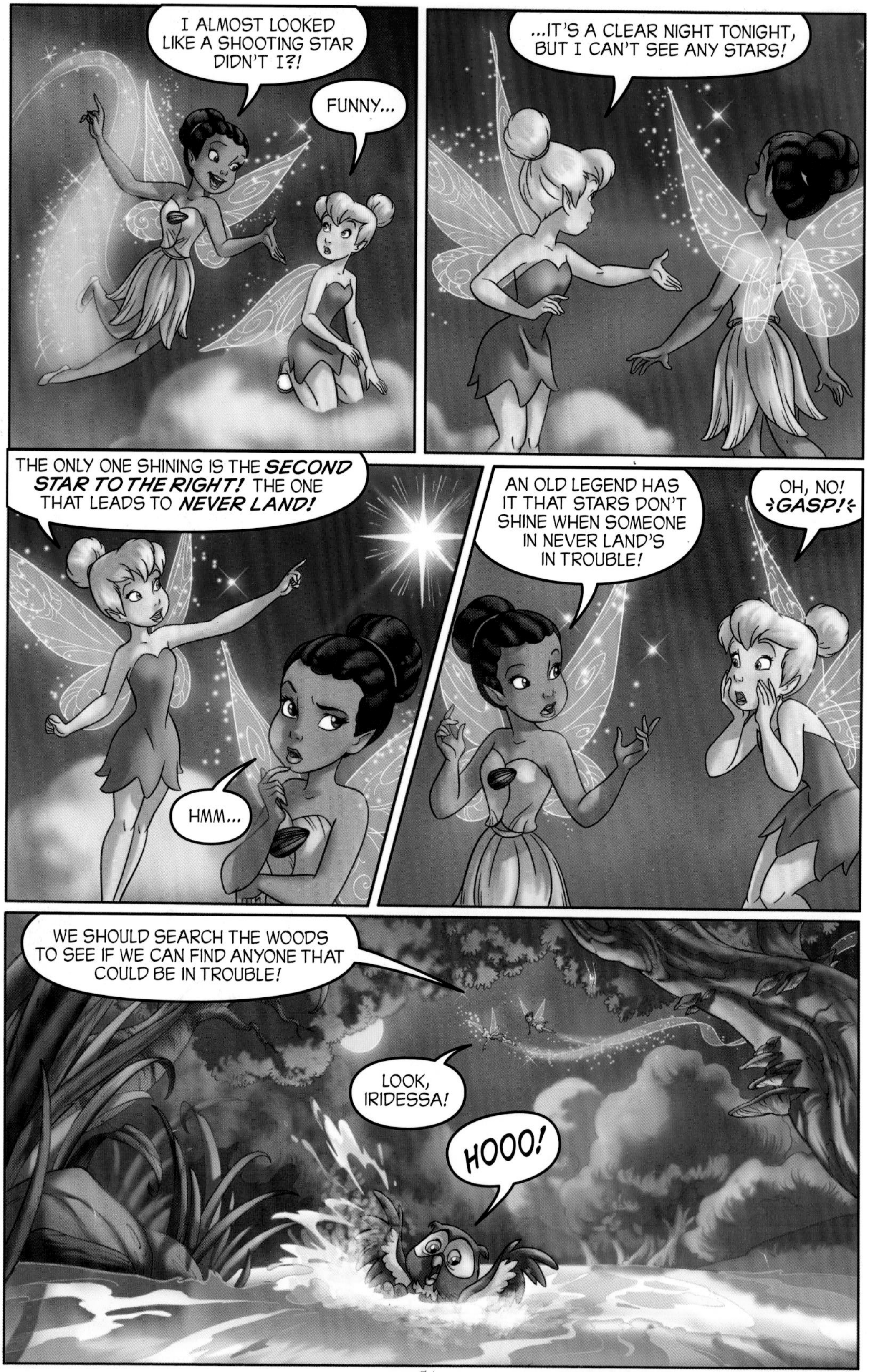
I ALMOST LOOKED LIKE A SHOOTING STAR DIDN'T I?!
FUNNY...
...IT'S A CLEAR NIGHT TONIGHT, BUT I CAN'T SEE ANY STARS!
THE ONLY ONE SHINING IS THE SECOND STAR TO THE RIGHT! THE ONE THAT LEADS TO NEVER LAND!
HMM...
AN OLD LEGEND HAS IT THAT STARS DON'T SHINE WHEN SOMEONE IN NEVER LAND'S IN TROUBLE!
OH, NO! GASP!
WE SHOULD SEARCH THE WOODS TO SEE IF WE CAN FIND ANYONE THAT COULD BE IN TROUBLE!
LOOK, IRIDESSA!
HOOO!

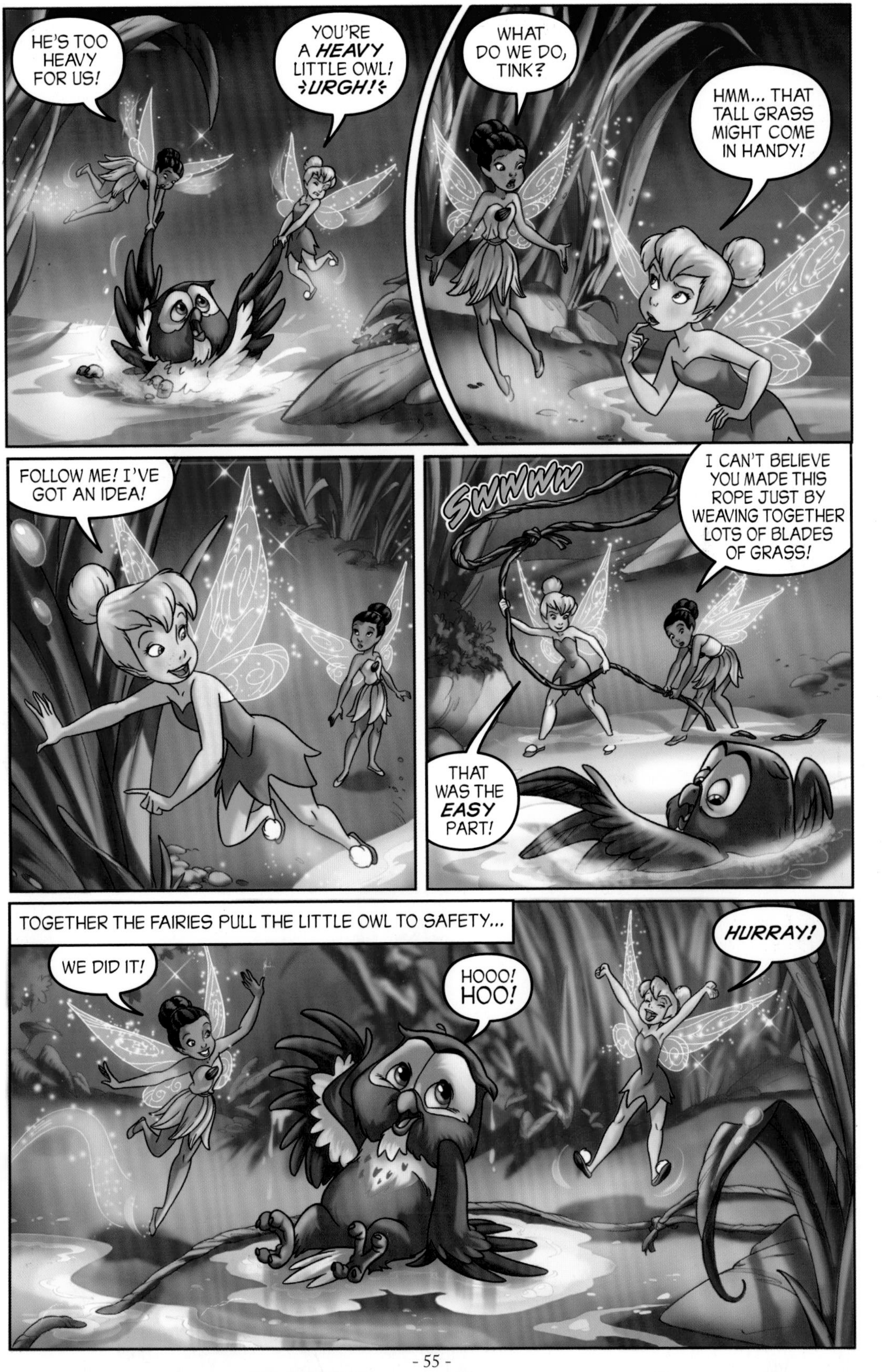
HE'S TOO HEAVY FOR US!
YOU'RE A *HEAVY* LITTLE OWL! *URGH!*
WHAT DO WE DO, TINK?
HMM... THAT TALL GRASS MIGHT COME IN HANDY!
FOLLOW ME! I'VE GOT AN IDEA!
SWWWW
I CAN'T BELIEVE YOU MADE THIS ROPE JUST BY WEAVING TOGETHER LOTS OF BLADES OF GRASS!
THAT WAS THE *EASY* PART!
TOGETHER THE FAIRIES PULL THE LITTLE OWL TO SAFETY...
WE DID IT!
HOOO! HOO!
HURRAY!

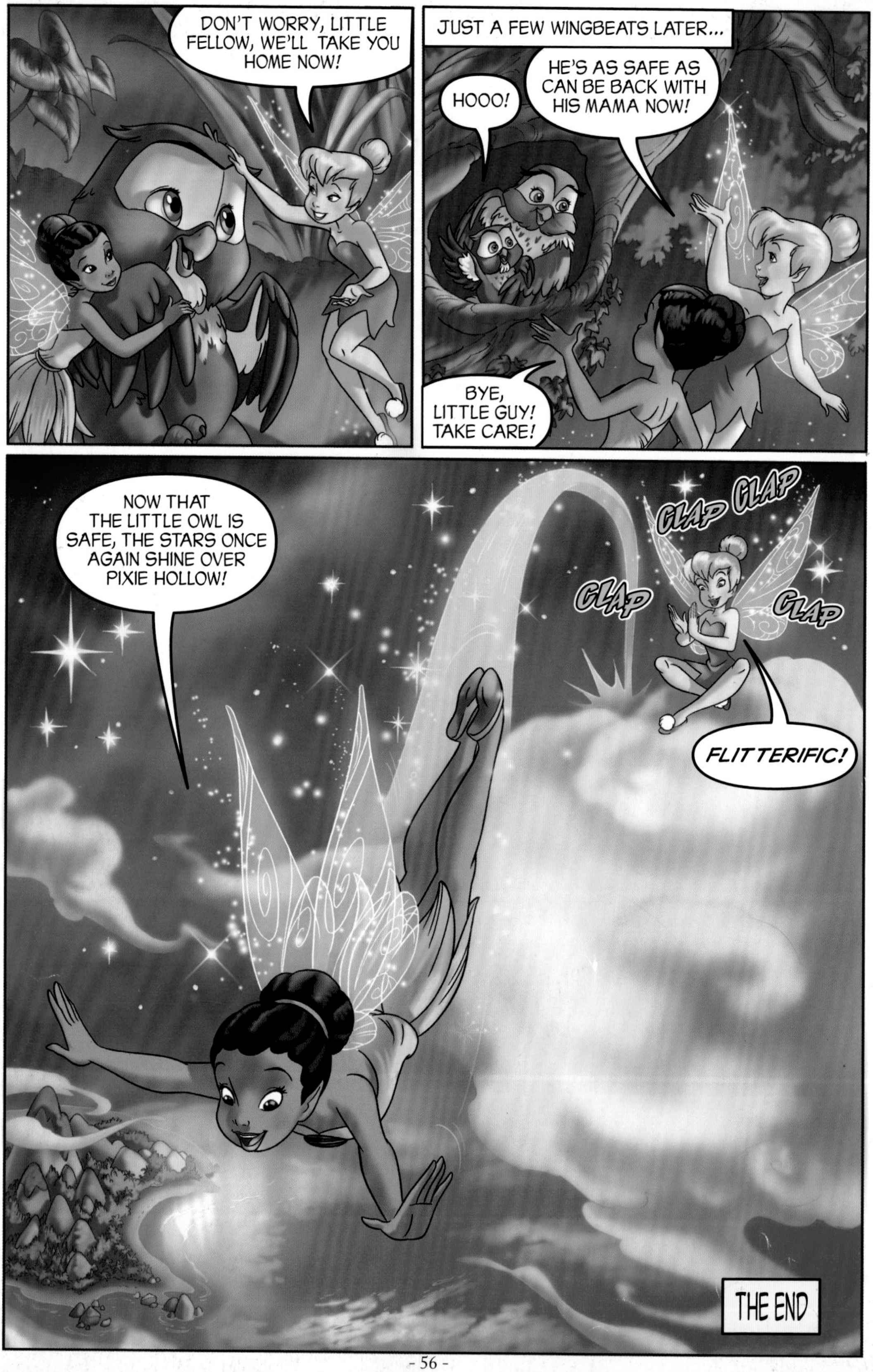
DON'T WORRY, LITTLE FELLOW, WE'LL TAKE YOU HOME NOW!
JUST A FEW WINGBEATS LATER...
HOOO!
HE'S AS SAFE AS CAN BE BACK WITH HIS MAMA NOW!
BYE, LITTLE GUY! TAKE CARE!
NOW THAT THE LITTLE OWL IS SAFE, THE STARS ONCE AGAIN SHINE OVER PIXIE HOLLOW!
CLAP CLAP
CLAP
CLAP
FLITTERIFIC!
THE END

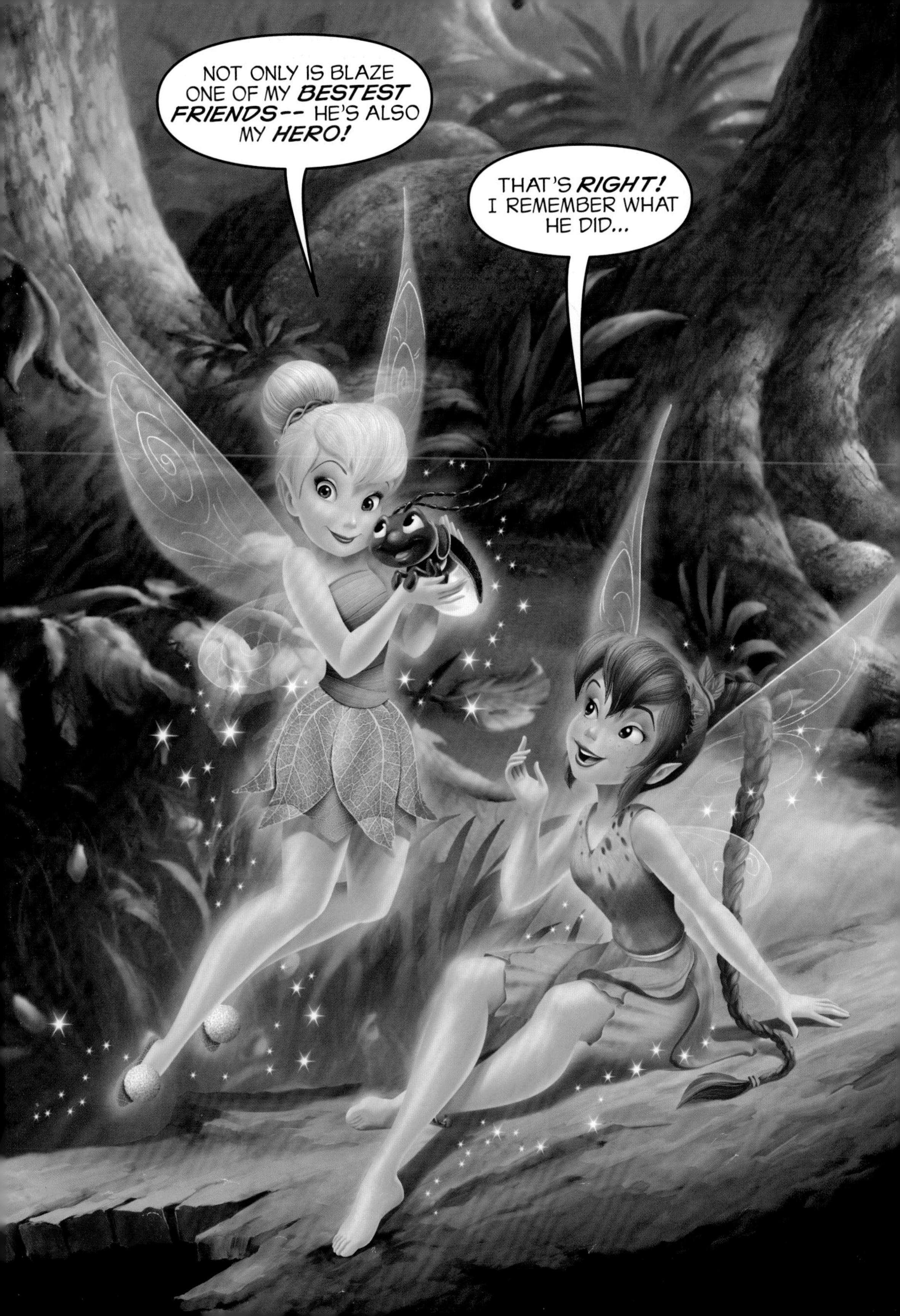
NOT ONLY IS BLAZE ONE OF MY BESTEST FRIENDS-- HE'S ALSO MY HERO!
THAT'S RIGHT! I REMEMBER WHAT HE DID...

AN UNEXPECTED ADVENTURE

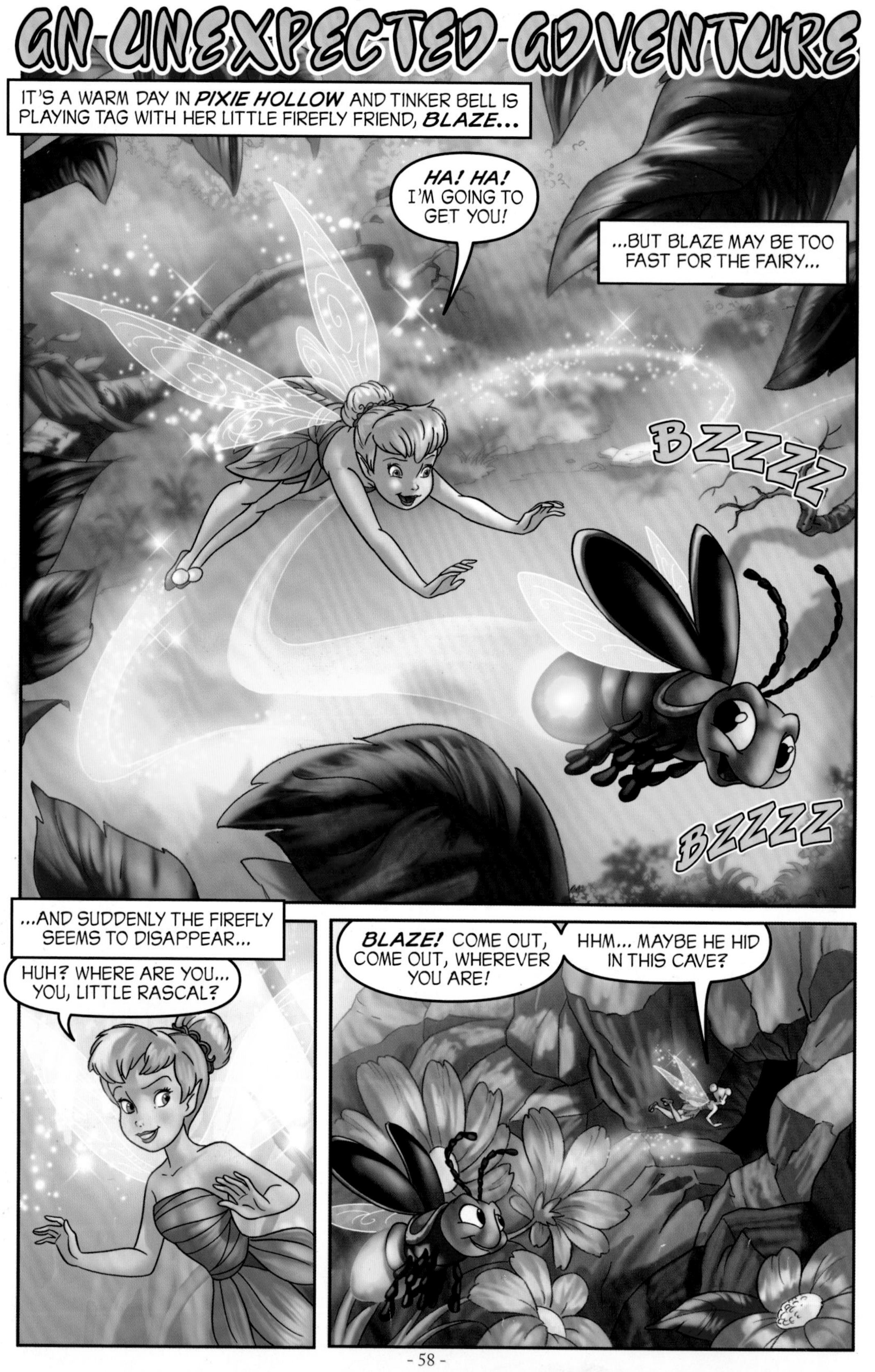

IT'S A WARM DAY IN *PIXIE HOLLOW* AND TINKER BELL IS PLAYING TAG WITH HER LITTLE FIREFLY FRIEND, *BLAZE...*
HA! HA! I'M GOING TO GET YOU!
...BUT BLAZE MAY BE TOO FAST FOR THE FAIRY...
BZZZZ
BZZZZ
...AND SUDDENLY THE FIREFLY SEEMS TO DISAPPEAR...
HUH? WHERE ARE YOU... YOU, LITTLE RASCAL?
BLAZE! COME OUT, COME OUT, WHEREVER YOU ARE!
HHM... MAYBE HE HID IN THIS CAVE?

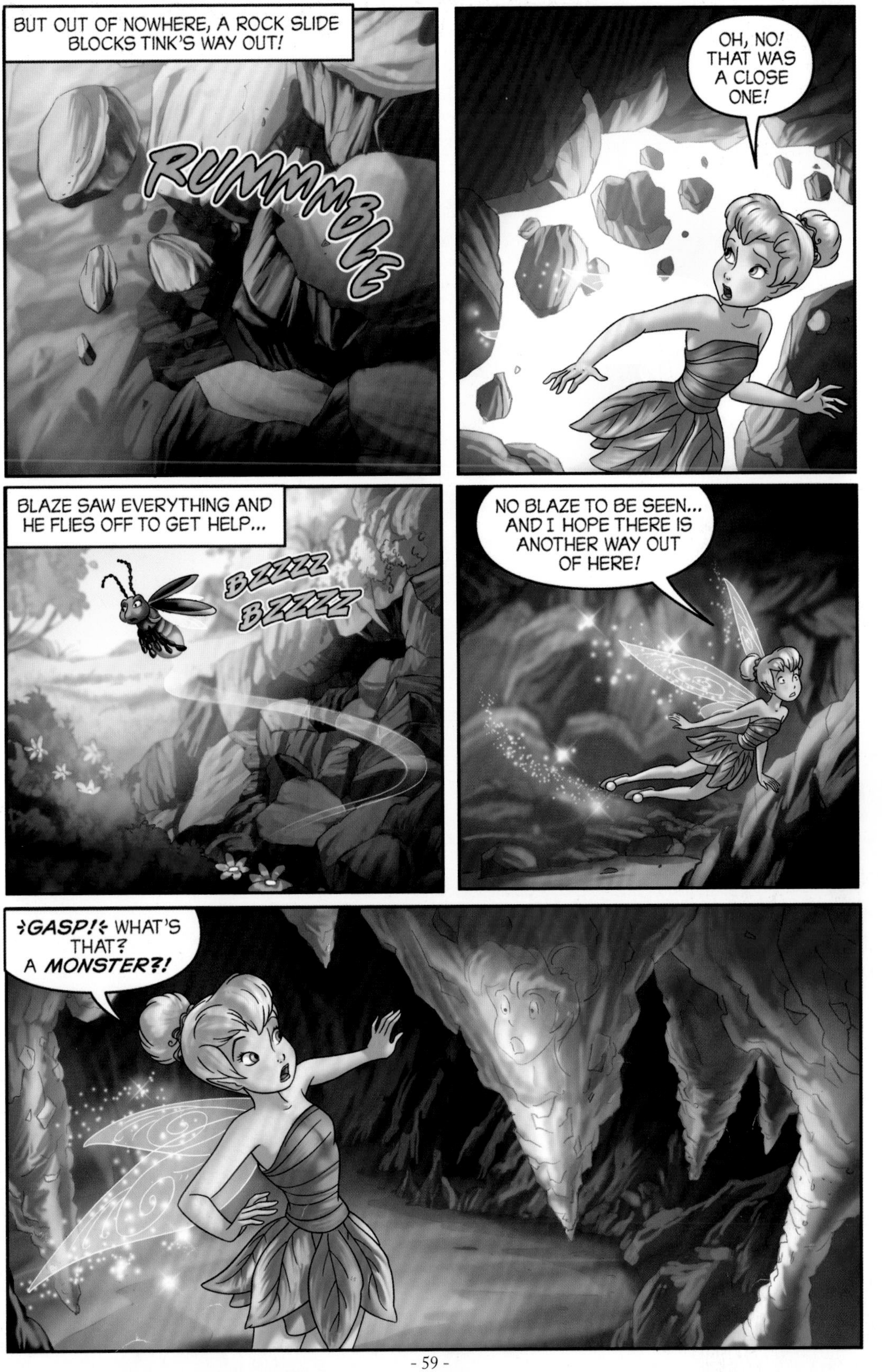
BUT OUT OF NOWHERE, A ROCK SLIDE BLOCKS TINK'S WAY OUT!
RUMMMBLE
OH, NO! THAT WAS A CLOSE ONE!
BLAZE SAW EVERYTHING AND HE FLIES OFF TO GET HELP...
BZZZZ BZZZZ
NO BLAZE TO BE SEEN... AND I HOPE THERE IS ANOTHER WAY OUT OF HERE!
GASP! WHAT'S THAT? A MONSTER?!

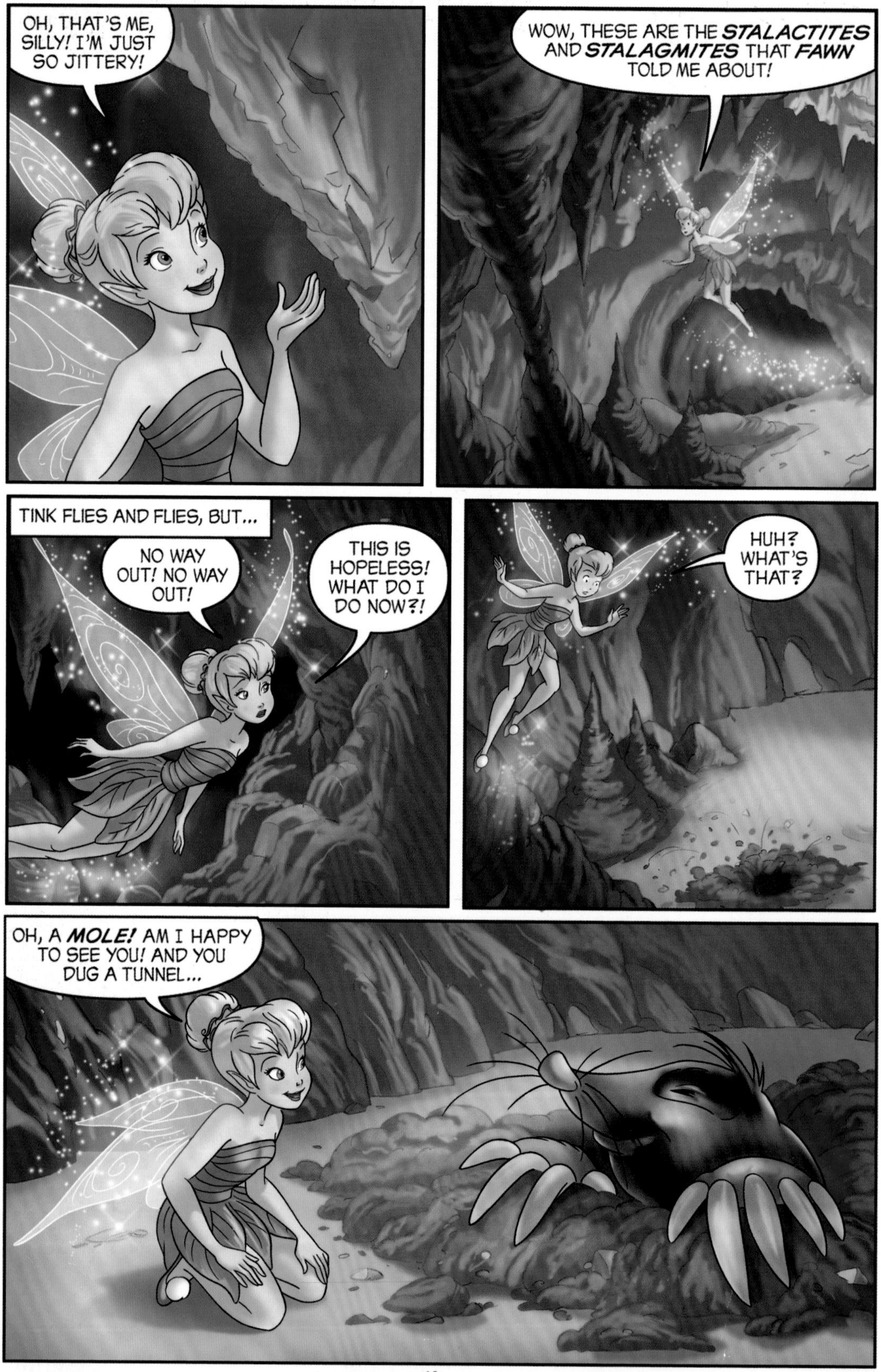

OH, THAT'S ME, SILLY! I'M JUST SO JITTERY!
WOW, THESE ARE THE STALACTITES AND STALAGMITES THAT FAWN TOLD ME ABOUT!
TINK FLIES AND FLIES, BUT...
NO WAY OUT! NO WAY OUT!
THIS IS HOPELESS! WHAT DO I DO NOW?!
HUH? WHAT'S THAT?
OH, A MOLE! AM I HAPPY TO SEE YOU! AND YOU DUG A TUNNEL...

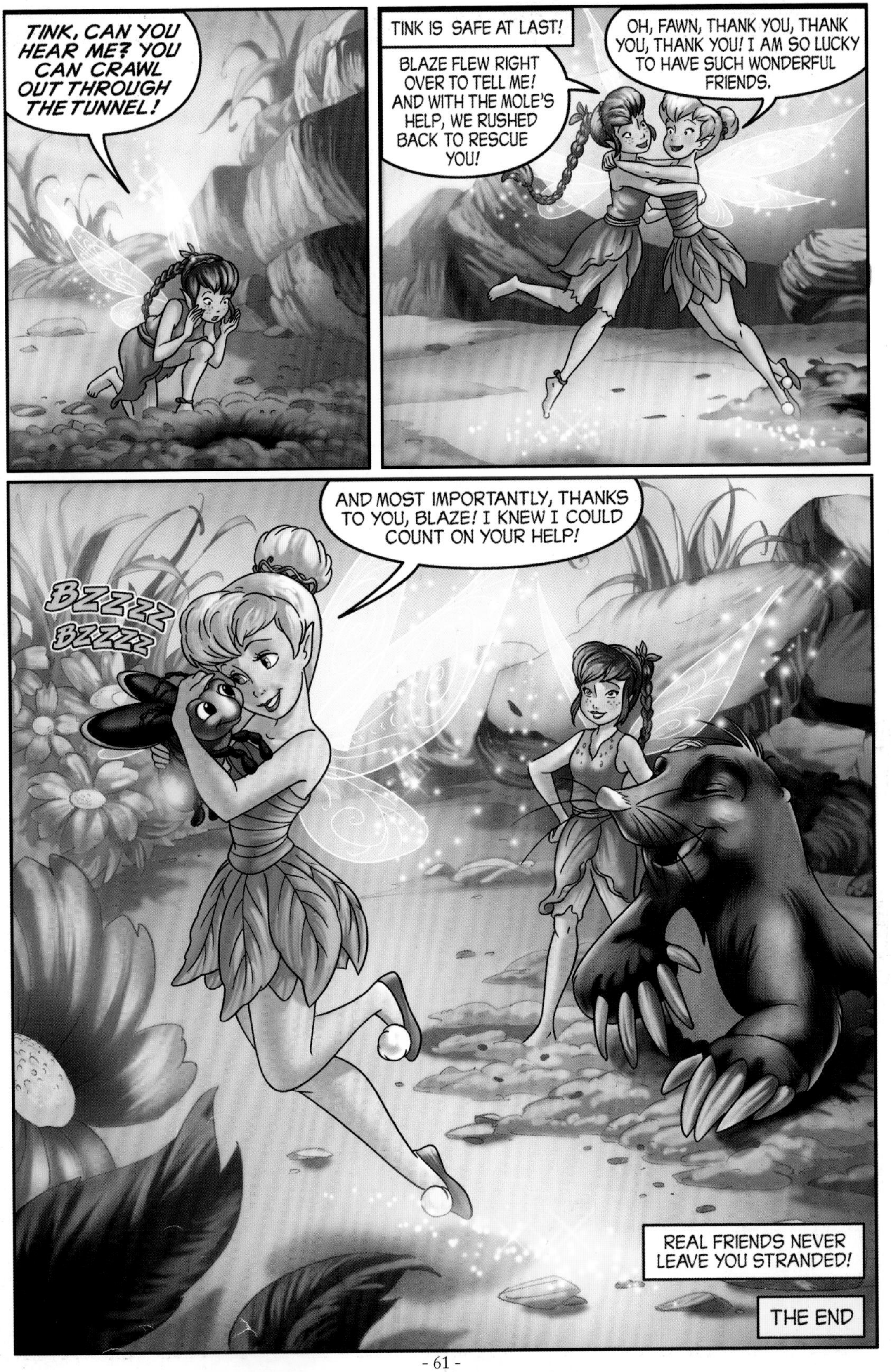
TINK, CAN YOU HEAR ME? YOU CAN CRAWL OUT THROUGH THE TUNNEL!
TINK IS SAFE AT LAST!
BLAZE FLEW RIGHT OVER TO TELL ME! AND WITH THE MOLE'S HELP, WE RUSHED BACK TO RESCUE YOU!
OH, FAWN, THANK YOU, THANK YOU, THANK YOU! I AM SO LUCKY TO HAVE SUCH WONDERFUL FRIENDS.
AND MOST IMPORTANTLY, THANKS TO YOU, BLAZE! I KNEW I COULD COUNT ON YOUR HELP!
BZZZZZ
BZZZZ
REAL FRIENDS NEVER LEAVE YOU STRANDED!
THE END

More Great Graphic Novels from PAPERCUTZ™

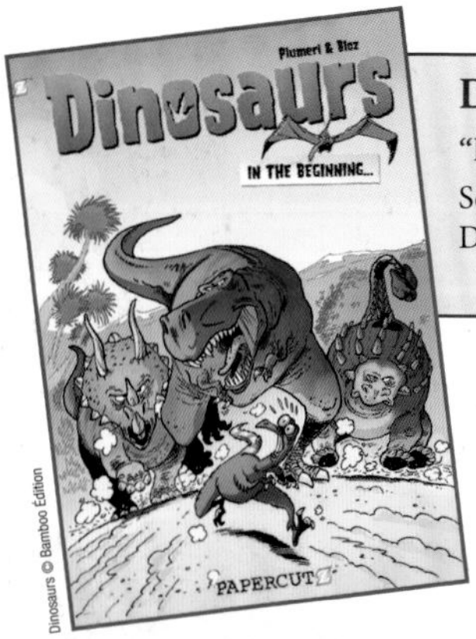
Plumeri & Bloz
Dinosaurs
IN THE BEGINNING...
PAPERCUTZ

DINOSAURS #1
"In the Beginning..."
Science facts combined with Dino-humor!

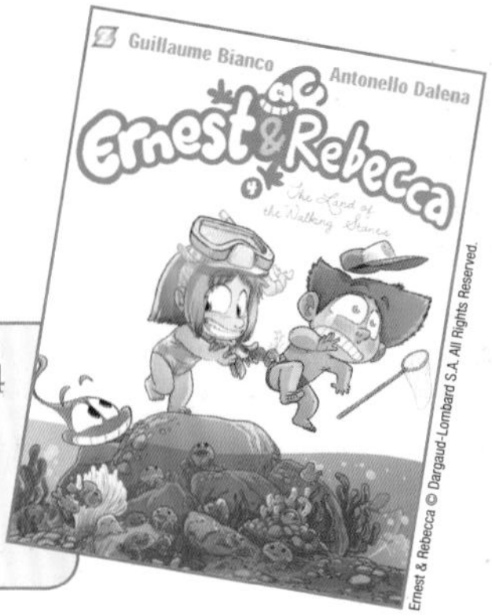
Guillaume Bianco
Antonello Dalena
Ernest & Rebecca

ERNEST & REBECCA #4
"The Land of Walking Stones"
A 6 ½ year old girl and her microbial buddy against the world!

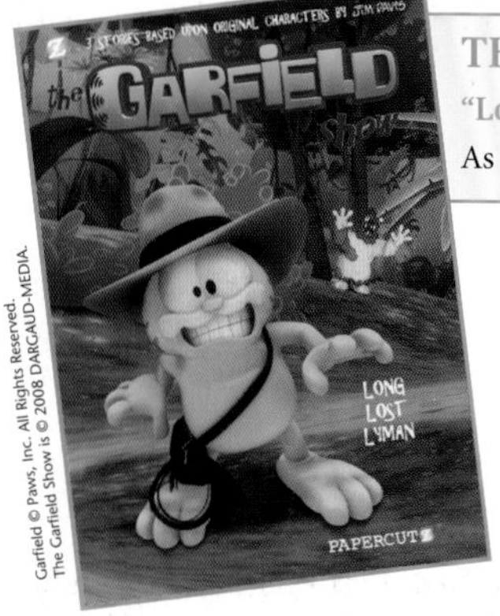
the GARFIELD Show
LONG LOST LYMAN
PAPERCUTZ

THE GARFIELD SHOW #3
"Long Lost Lyman"
As seen on the Cartoon Network!

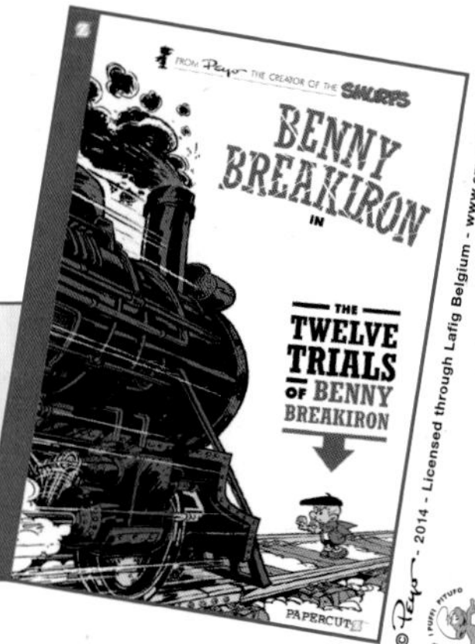
BENNY BREAKIRON IN
THE TWELVE TRIALS OF BENNY BREAKIRON
PAPERCUTZ

BENNY BREAKIRON #3
"The Twelve Trials of Benny Breakiron"
Benny Breakiron goes on the trip of a lifetime in his newest adventure!

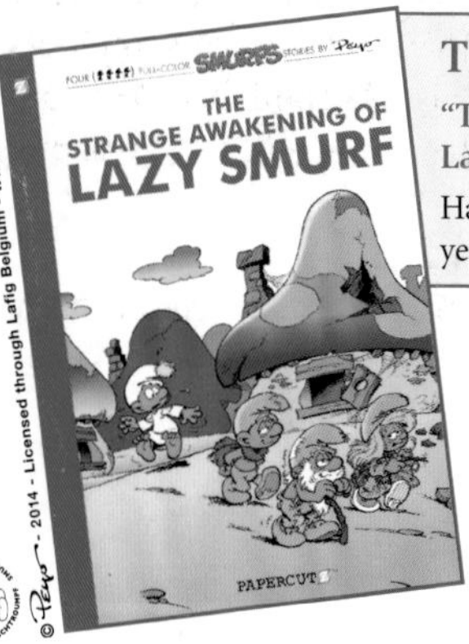
THE STRANGE AWAKENING OF LAZY SMURF
PAPERCUTZ

THE SMURFS #17
"The Strange Awakening of Lazy Smurf"
Has Lazy Smurf been asleep for 200 years?

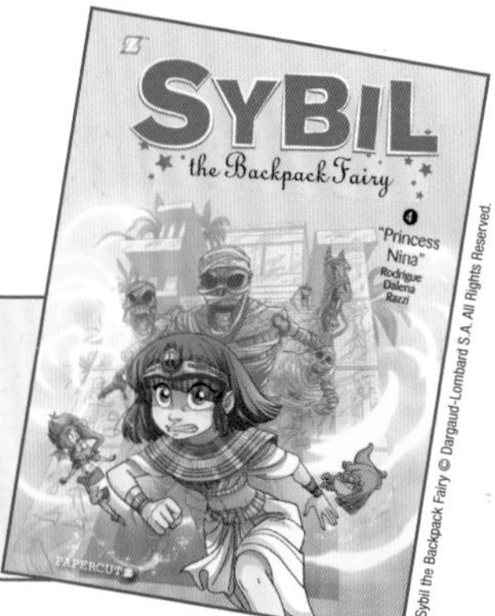
SYBIL
the Backpack Fairy
"Princess Nina"
PAPERCUTZ

SYBIL THE BACKPACK FAIRY #4
"Princess Nina"
Nina and Sybil's Excellent Adventure Through Time!

Available at better booksellers everywhere!

Or order directly from us! DINOSAURS is available in hardcover only for $10.99; ERNEST & REBECCA is $11.99 in hardcover only; THE GARFIELD SHOW is available in paperback for $7.99, in hardcover for $11.99; BENNY BREAKIRON is available in hardcover only for $11.99; THE SMURFS are available in paperback for $5.99, in hardcover for $10.99; and SYBIL THE BACKPACK FAIRY is available in hardcover only for $10.99.

Please add $4.00 for postage and handling for the first book, add $1.00 for each additional book.

Please make check payable to NBM Publishing. Send to: PAPERCUTZ, 160 Broadway, Suite 700, East Wing, New York, NY 10038 (1-800-886-1223)

WATCH OUT FOR PAPERCUTZ

Tinker Bell
An Evolution
Mindy Johnson
Foreword by John Lasseter

Welcome to the fairy-filled fourteenth DISNEY FAIRIES graphic novel from Papercutz, those pint-size pixies dedicated to publishing great graphic novels for all ages! I'm Jim Salicrup, the full-time Editor-in-Chief, and part-time Fairy Aficionado around here!

Normally in this space I try to tell you a little bit about what else is happening in the wonderful world of Papercutz, but this time around, I have something else so exciting to tell you about, you'll just have to visit Papercutz.com to find out what's new and exciting at your favorite graphic novel publisher for all ages!

It's even possible you may already know what I'm going to tell you! After all, you probably love Tinker Bell just as much, possibly even more, than I do! Recently, an amazing new book came out all about the real-life history of our favorite Never Land fairy—"Tinker Bell: An Evolution" by Mindy Johnson and published by Disney Editions Deluxe. When I saw this beautiful book on the bookstore shelves, I knew I just had to have it! It's filled from cover-to-cover with fascinating facts and awesome artwork, all about how Tinker Bell was originally created and how she evolved to be the Pixie Hollow fairy we all know and love today.

What kind of facts? Well, for example… "How did Tinker Bell get her name? In J. M. Barrie's original version of the play 'Peter Pan,' the little sprite's name was Tippytoe, and she had speaking lines. But over time, Barrie decided that the fairy's expressions would be best voiced by musical chimes. During the early 1900s, vagabonds known as tinkers traveled from town to town, performing jack-of-all-trade repair services. Their arrival was hailed by the jingling of bells fashioned from tin that they mounted on their wagons. One of these 'tinker bells' was used to give Peter's fairy friend her voice in the original stage production, and the name stuck."

And there's so much more to be found in "Tinker Bell: An Evolution." If you're as curious about the history of Tinker Bell as I am, this is the book for you! Check either your favorite bookseller or library and ask to see a copy yourself. I know you'll love it!

In the meantime, keep believing in "faith, trust, and pixie dust"!

Thanks,

Jim

STAY IN TOUCH!

EMAIL:	salicrup@papercutz.com
WEB:	www.papercutz.com
TWITTER:	@papercutzgn
FACEBOOK:	PAPERCUTZGRAPHICNOVELS
REGULAR MAIL:	Papercutz, 160 Broadway, Suite 700, East Wing, New York, NY 10038

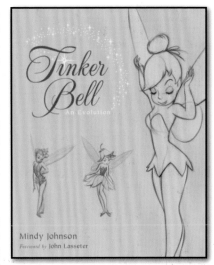

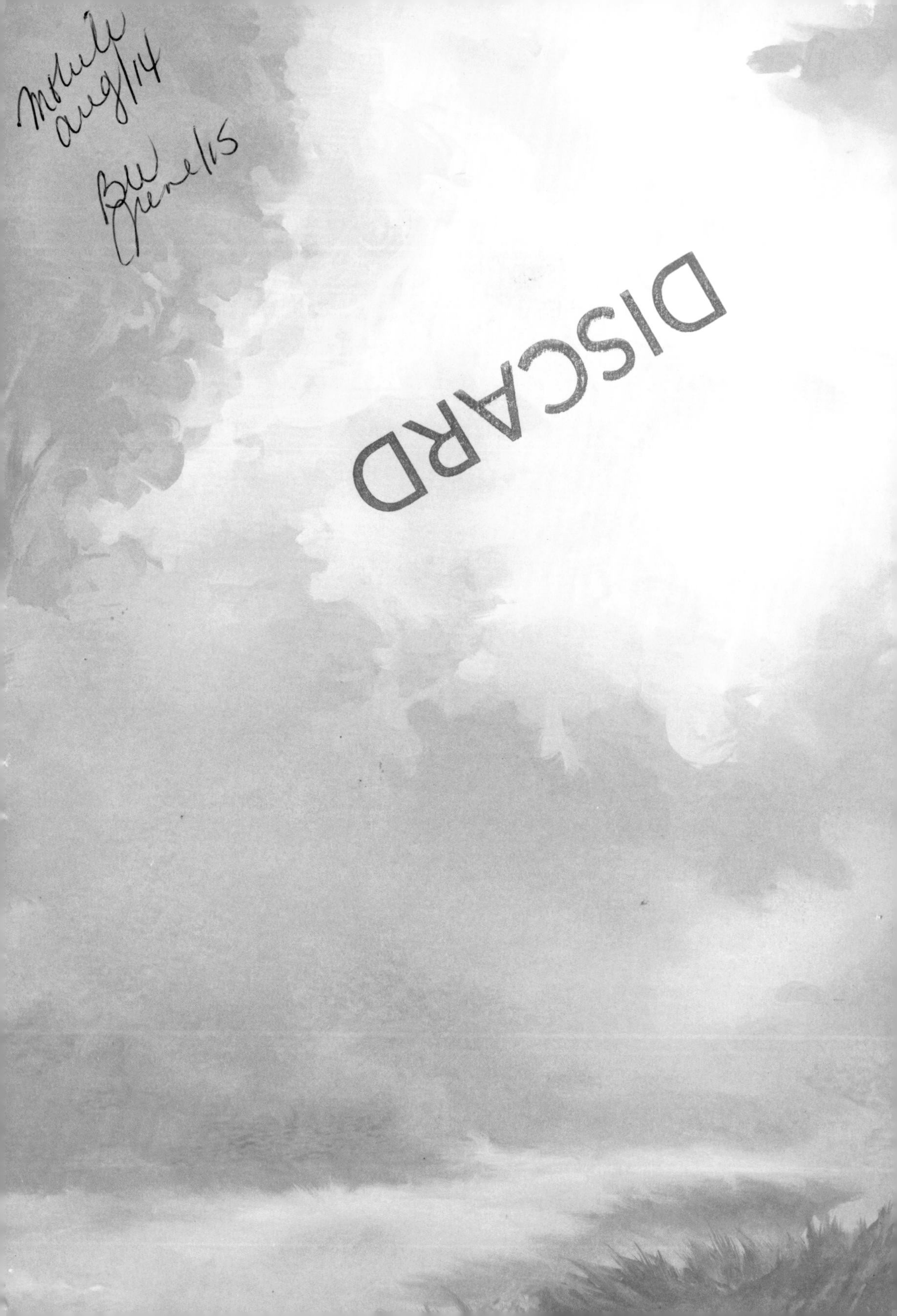